Glad Tidings

A CHRISTMAS READER

Glad Tidings

A CHRISTMAS READER

Edited by Carol Kelly-Gangi

BARNES
& NOBLE
BOOKS
NEW YORK

Glad Tidings is an expanded edition of *A Christmas Anthology*
(1999, Barnes & Noble Books).

2000 Barnes & Noble Books

ISBN 0-7607-2335-4

Book design by Jennifer Ann Daddio

Printed and bound in the United States of America

00 01 02 03 04 MC 9 8 7 6 5 4 3 2 1

QH

Contents

Glad Tidings

A CHRISTMAS READER

Introduction

If you're anything like me, you invariably run out of time during the Christmas season. Despite my best intentions, I've spent many a Christmas Eve wrapping gifts into the wee hours of the morning, thinking "if I only had another day." Still, taking time out to reflect on all that is Christmas may be the perfect antidote to holiday mania. That more than 10,000 books with "Christmas" in the title line the shelves of the Library of Congress suggests that the writing—and reading—of words inspired by the season has a rich history all its own.

In *Glad Tidings*, an expanded edition of *A Christmas Anthology*, we've reached further backward and forward in time than in our original collection to capture a broader array of Christmas writings. Each of these works—which were written in periods ranging from the early Middle Ages to the early 1990s—was chosen for its insight into the traditional Christmas experience. The diversity of viewpoints as to just what that experience is should not surprise anyone.

Some contributors focus on a memorable Christmas in their own lives. In "My Christmas Miracle," popular novelist Taylor Caldwell recalls her own "truest" Christmas. She describes a bleak time in her life when a random act of kindness to a stranger was repaid in ways that restored her faith in the message of Christmas—and in herself. Pulitzer Prize-winning author Hamlin Garland harkens back to his childhood in the Wisconsin coulée to reminisce about the night he saw his first Christmas tree and a time when "a keen appetite and empty hands" were his only contributions to the festivities.

For some, the holidays are the only time in the year when their family comes together. Family is another recurring theme in the book. Despite minor stresses and strains, it goes without saying that it's within the company of our loved ones that most of us experience Christmas and preserve its memories. Such perennial classics as O. Henry's "The Gift of the Magi" and an excerpt from Louisa May Alcott's *Little Women* have been included in the collection, as well as more contemporary pieces devoted to family and Christmas. In "Christmas Day in the Morning," Nobel Prize-winner Pearl S. Buck tells the story of a man whose memory of a gift he gave his father more than forty years before rekindles in him the magic of Christmas. Rita Dove, Poet Laureate of 1993, contributes "My Father's Telescope," a touching poem about a father's efforts to fashion a gift for his son. And novelist Terry Kay fondly recalls the Christmas his daughter received a favorite doll in "Gift Rap"—a whimsical lament over the commercialization of the holiday.

Other stories reveal a painful reality behind the holiday cheer. In Langston Hughes's "One Christmas Eve," a black child comes to a sobering realization amid the season's festivities in 1930s America, and Ring Lardner's "Old Folks' Christmas" presents a family who have outgrown their holiday traditions altogether.

Exploring the traditional symbols of the season, Robert Frost and Hans Christian Andersen write poignantly of

Christmas trees, and Henry Wadsworth Longfellow attunes himself to the "wild and sweet" pealing of Christmas bells. The fleeting figure of Santa Claus is the subject of Clement Clarke Moore's holiday classic "A Visit from St. Nicholas," while Francis P. Church's public letter to a young girl, "Yes Virginia, There Is a Santa Claus," affirms the permanence of the Christmas spirit. Other writers pay tribute to the ultimate symbol of the season—the Nativity scene. Robert Stephen Hawker, Margaret Deland, Elizabeth Madox Roberts, and Edgar Guest catch the softly breathing animals and awestruck shepherds present on that first Christmas Eve—and reflect, as does Thomas Hardy, on what our own reaction would be to such a strange and wondrous sight.

And what Christmas concoction would be complete without a helping of Dickens. Here, we offer "Marley's Ghost," Stave I from the classic tale *A Christmas Carol*, in which Ebenezer Scrooge experiences his first shudder of a haunting Christmas lesson.

Rounding out the anthology is a selection of ancient English ballads and traditional carols—we hope your favorite is here!—and a sampling of time-honored recipes for savory holiday foods from Fannie Merritt Farmer's *The Boston Cooking-School Cook Book*.

At a festive party, in front of a blazing fire—or enjoying Christmas in your own special way—we hope *Glad Tidings* will make your spirits even brighter still.

—Carol Kelly-Gangi
New York, New York
2000

My Christmas Miracle

TAYLOR CALDWELL

For many of us, one Christmas stands out from all the others, the one when the meaning of the day shone clearest.

Although I did not guess it, my own "truest" Christmas began on a rainy spring day in the bleakest year of my life. Recently divorced, I was in my 20s, had no job, and was on my way downtown to go the rounds of the employment offices. I had no umbrella, for my old one had fallen apart, and I could not afford another one. I sat down in the streetcar, and there against the seat was a beautiful silk umbrella with a silver handle inlaid with gold and flecks of bright enamel. I had never seen anything so lovely.

I examined the handle and saw a name engraved among the golden scrolls. The usual procedure would have been to turn in the umbrella to the conductor, but on impulse I decided to take it with me and find the owner myself. I got off the streetcar in a downpour and thankfully opened the umbrella to protect myself. Then I searched a telephone book for the name on the umbrella and found it. I called, and a lady answered.

Yes, she said in surprise, that was her umbrella, which her parents, now dead, had given her for a birthday present. But, she added, it had been stolen from her locker at school (she was a teacher) more than a year before. She was so excited that I forgot I was looking for a job and went directly to her small house. She took the umbrella, and her eyes filled with tears.

The teacher wanted to give me a reward, but—though $20 was all I had in the world—her happiness at retrieving this special possession was such that to have accepted money would have spoiled something. We talked for a while, and I must have given her my address. I don't remember.

The next six months were wretched. I was able to obtain only temporary employment here and there, for a small salary, though this was what they now call the Roaring Twenties. But I put aside 25 or 50 cents when I could afford it for my little girl's Christmas presents. (It took me six months to save $8.) My last job ended the day before Christmas, my $30 rent was soon due, and I had $15 to my name—which Peggy and I would need for food. She was home from her convent boarding school and was excitedly looking forward to her gifts the next day, which I had already purchased. I had bought her a small tree, and we were going to decorate it that night.

The stormy air was full of the sound of Christmas merriment as I walked from the streetcar to my small apartment. Bells rang and children shouted in the bitter dusk of the evening, and windows were lighted and everyone was running and laughing. But there would be no Christmas for me, I knew, no gifts, no remembrance whatsoever. As I struggled through the snowdrifts, I just about reached the lowest point in my life. Unless a miracle happened I would be homeless in January, foodless, jobless. I had prayed steadily for weeks, and there had been no answer but this coldness and darkness, this harsh air, this abandonment. God and men had completely forgotten me. I felt old as death, and as lonely. What was to become of us?

I looked in my mailbox. There were only bills in it, a sheaf of them, and two white envelopes which I was sure contained more bills. I went up three dusty flights of stairs, and I cried, shivering in my thin coat. But I made myself smile so I could greet my little daughter with a pretense of happiness. She opened the door for me and threw herself in my arms, screaming joyously and demanding that we decorate the tree immediately.

Peggy was not yet six years old, and had been alone all day while I worked. She had set our kitchen table for our evening meal, proudly, and put pans out and the three cans of food which would be our dinner. For some reason, when I looked at those pans and cans, I felt brokenhearted. We would have only hamburgers for our Christmas dinner tomorrow, and gelatin. I stood in the cold little kitchen, and misery overwhelmed me. For the first time in my life, I doubted the existence of God and His mercy, and the coldness in my heart was colder than ice.

The doorbell rang, and Peggy ran fleetly to answer it, calling that it must be Santa Claus. Then I heard a man talking heartily to her and went to the door. He was a delivery man, and his arms were full of big parcels, and he was laughing at my child's frenzied joy and her dancing. "This is a mistake," I said, but he read the name on the parcels, and they were for me. When he had gone I could only stare at the boxes. Peggy and I sat on the floor and opened them. A huge doll, three times the size of the one I had bought for her. Gloves. Candy. A beautiful leather purse. Incredible! I looked for the name of the sender. It was the teacher, the address simply "California," where she had moved.

Our dinner that night was the most delicious I had ever eaten. I could only pray in myself, "Thank You, Father." I forgot I had no money for the rent and only $15 in my purse and no job. My child and I ate and laughed together in happiness. Then we decorated the little tree and marveled at it. I put Peggy to bed and set up her gifts around the tree, and a sweet peace flooded me like a benediction. I had some hope again. I could even examine the sheaf of bills without cringing. Then I opened the two white envelopes. One contained a check for $30 from a company I had worked for briefly in the summer. It was, said a note, my "Christmas bonus." My rent!

The other envelope was an offer of a permanent position with the government—to begin two days after Christmas. I sat with the letter in my hand and the check on the table before me, and I think that was the most joyful moment of my life up to that time.

The church bells began to ring. I hurriedly looked at my child, who was sleeping blissfully, and ran down to the street. Everywhere people were walking to church to celebrate the birth of the Saviour. People smiled at me and I smiled back. The storm had stopped, the sky was pure and glittering with stars.

"The Lord is born!" sang the bells to the crystal night and the laughing darkness. Someone began to sing, "Come, all ye faithful!" I joined in and sang with the strangers all about me.

I am not alone at all, I thought. *I was never alone at all.*

And that, of course, is the message of Christmas. We are never alone. Not when the night is darkest, the wind coldest, the world seemingly most indifferent. For this is still the time God chooses.

The Christmas Silence

Hushed are the pigeons cooing low,
On dusty rafters of the loft;
And mild-eyed oxen, breathing soft,
Sleep on the fragrant hay below.

Dim shadows in the corners hide;
The glimmering lantern's rays are shed,
Where one young lamb just lifts his head
Then huddles against his mother's side.

Strange silence tingles in the air;
Through the half-open door a bar
Of light from one low hanging star
Touches a baby's radiant hair—

No sound—The mother, kneeling, lays
Her cheek against the little face.
Oh, human love! Oh, heavenly grace!
Tis yet in silence that she prays!

Ages of silence end to-night;
Then to the long expectant earth
Glad angels come to greet His birth
In burst of music, love and light!

MARGARET DELAND

A Christmas Carol

The Christ-child lay on Mary's lap,
His hair was like a light.
(O weary, weary were the world,
But here is all aright.)

The Christ-child lay on Mary's breast,
His hair was like a star.
(O stern and cunning are the kings,
But here the true hearts are.)

The Christ-child lay on Mary's heart,
His hair was like a fire.
(O weary, weary is the world,
But here the world's desire.)

The Christ-child stood at Mary's knee,
His hair was like a crown,
And all the flowers looked up at Him,
And all the stars looked down.

G. K. CHESTERTON

My First Christmas Tree

HAMLIN GARLAND

I will begin by saying that we never had a Christmas tree in our house in the Wisconsin coulée; indeed, my father never saw one in a family circle till he saw that which I set up for my own children last year. But we celebrated Christmas in those days, always, and I cannot remember a time when we did not all hang up our stockings for "Sandy Claws" to fill. As I look back upon those days it seems as if the snows were always deep, the night skies crystal clear, and the stars especially lustrous with frosty sparkles of blue and yellow fire—and probably this was so, for we lived in a Northern land where winter was usually stern and always long.

I recall one Christmas when "Sandy" brought me a sled, and a horse that stood on rollers—a wonderful tin horse which I very shortly split in two in order to see what his insides were. Father traded a cord of wood for the sled, and the horse cost twenty cents—but they made the day wonderful.

Another notable Christmas Day, as I stood in our front yard, mid-leg deep in snow, a neighbor drove by closely muffled in furs, while behind his seat his son, a lad of twelve or fifteen, stood beside a barrel of apples, and as he passed he hurled a glorious big red one at me. It missed me, but bored a deep, round hole in the soft snow. I thrill yet with the remembered joy of burrowing for that delicious bomb. Nothing will ever smell quite as good as that Wine Sap or Northern Spy or whatever it was. It was a wayward impulse on the part of the boy in the sleigh, but it warms my heart after more than forty years.

We had no chimney in our home, but the stocking-hanging was a ceremony nevertheless. My parents, and especially my mother, entered into it with the best of humor. They always put up their own stockings or permitted us to do it for them—and they always laughed next morning when they found potatoes or ears of corn in them. I can see now that my mother's laugh had a tear in it, for she loved pretty things and seldom got any during the years that we lived in the coulée.

When I was ten years old we moved to Mitchell County, an Iowa prairie land, and there we prospered in such wise that our stockings always held toys of some sort, and even my mother's stocking occasionally sagged with a simple piece of jewelry or a new comb or brush. But the thought of a family tree remained the luxury of millionaire city dwellers;

indeed it was not till my fifteenth or sixteenth year that our Sunday school rose to the extravagance of a tree, and it is of this wondrous festival that I write.

The land about us was only partly cultivated at this time, and our district schoolhouse, a bare little box, was set bleakly on the prairie; but the Burr Oak schoolhouse was not only larger but it stood beneath great oaks as well and possessed the charm of a forest background through which a stream ran silently. It was our chief social center. There on a Sunday a regular preacher held "Divine service" with Sunday school as a sequence. At night—usually on Friday nights—the young people let in "ly-ceums," as we called them, to debate great questions or to "speak pieces" and read essays; and here it was that I saw my first Christmas tree.

I walked to that tree across four miles of moonlit snow. Snow? No, it was a floor of diamonds, a magical world, so beautiful that my heart still aches with the wonder of it and with the regret that it has all gone—gone with the keen eyes and the bounding pulses of the boy.

Our home at this time was a small frame house on the prairie almost directly west of the Burr Oak grove, and as it was too cold to take the horses out my brother and I, with our tall boots, our visored caps and our long woolen mufflers, started forth afoot defiant of the cold. We left the gate on the trot, bound for a sight of the glittering unknown. The snow was deep and we moved side by side in the grooves made by the hoofs of the horses, setting our feet in the shine left by the broad shoes of the wood sleighs whose going had smoothed the way for us.

Our breaths rose like smoke in the still air. It must have been ten below zero, but that did not trouble us in those days, and at last we came in sight of the lights, in sound of the singing, the laughter, the bells of the feast.

It was a poor little building without tower or bell and its low walls had but three windows on a side, and yet it seemed very imposing to me that night as I crossed the threshold and faced the strange people who packed it to the door. I say "strange people," for though I had seen most of them many times they all seemed somehow alien to me that night. I was an irregular attendant at Sunday school and did not expect a present, therefore I stood against the wall and gazed with open-eyed marveling at the shining pine which stood where the pulpit was wont to be. I was made to feel the more embarrassed by reason of the remark of a boy who accused me of having forgotten to comb my hair.

This was not true, but the cap I wore always matted my hair down over my brow, and then, when I lifted it off invariably disarranged it completely. Nevertheless I felt guilty—and hot. I don't suppose my hair was artistically barbered that night—I rather guess Mother had used the shears—and I can believe that I looked the half-wild colt that I was; but there was no call for that youth to direct attention to my unavoidable shagginess.

I don't think the tree had many candles, and I don't remember that it glittered with golden apples. But it was loaded with presents, and the girls coming and going clothed in bright garments made me forget my own looks—I think they made me forget to remove my overcoat, which was a sodden thing of poor cut and worse quality. I think I must have stood agape for nearly two hours listening to the songs, noting every motion of Adoniram Burtch and Asa Walker as they directed the ceremonies and prepared the way for the great event—that is to say, for the coming of Santa Claus himself.

A furious jingling of bells, a loud voice outside, the lifting of a window, the nearer clash of bells, and the dear old Saint appeared (in the person of Stephen Bartle) clothed in a red robe, a belt of sleigh bells, and a long white beard. The children cried out, "Oh!" The girls tittered and shrieked with excitement, and the boys laughed and clapped their hands. Then "Sandy" made a little speech about being glad to see us all, but as he had many other places to visit, and as there were a great many presents to distribute, he guessed he'd have to ask some of the many pretty girls to help him. So he called upon Betty Burtch and Hattie Knapp—and I for one admired his taste, for they were the most popular maids of the school.

They came up blushing, and a little bewildered by the blaze of publicity thus blown upon them. But their native dignity asserted itself, and the distribution of the presents began. I have a notion now that the fruit upon the tree was mostly bags of popcorn and "corny copias" of candy, but as my brother and I stood there that night and saw everybody, even the rowdiest boy, getting something we felt aggrieved and rebellious. We forgot that we had come from afar—we only knew that we were being left out.

But suddenly, in the midst of our gloom, my brother's

name was called, and a lovely girl with a gentle smile handed him a bag of popcorn. My heart glowed with gratitude. Somebody had thought of us; and when she came to me, saying sweetly, "Here's something for you," I had not words to thank her. This happened nearly forty years ago, but her smile, her outstretched hand, her sympathetic eyes are vividly before me as I write. She was sorry for the shock-headed boy who stood against the wall, and her pity made the little box of candy a casket of pearls. The fact that I swallowed the jewels on the road home does not take from the reality of my adoration.

At last I had to take my final glimpse of that wondrous tree, and I well remember the walk home. My brother and I traveled in wordless companionship. The moon was sinking toward the west, and the snow crust gleamed with a million fairy lamps. The sentinel watchdogs barked from lonely farm-houses, and the wolves answered from the ridges. Now and then sleighs passed us with lovers sitting two and two, and the bells on their horses had the remote music of romance to us whose boots drummed like clogs of wood upon the icy road.

Our house was dark as we approached and entered it, but how deliciously warm it seemed after the pitiless wind! I confess we made straight for the cupboard for a mince pie, a doughnut and a bowl of milk!

As I write this there stands in my library a thick-branched, beautifully tapering fir tree covered with the gold and purple apples of Hesperides, together with crystal ice points, green and red and yellow candles, clusters of gilded grapes, wreaths of metallic frost, and glittering angels swinging in ecstasy; but I doubt if my children will ever know the keen pleasure (that is almost pain) which came to my brother and to me in those Christmas days when an orange was not a breakfast fruit, but a casket of incense and of spice, a message from the sunlands of the South.

That was our compensation—we brought to our Christmastime a keen appetite and empty hands. And the lesson of it all is, if we are seeking a lesson, that it is better to give to those who want than to those for whom "we ought to do something because they did something for us last year."

O Holy Night

O holy night, the stars are brightly shining;
It is the night of the dear Saviour's birth.
Long lay the world in sin and error pining,
Till He appeared and the soul felt its worth.
A thrill of hope, the weary world rejoices,
For yonder breaks a new and glorious morn.
Fall on your knees!
Oh, hear the angel voices!
O night divine!
O night when Christ was born!
O night divine!
O night, O night divine!

CAPPEAU DE ROQUEMAURE
Translated by John S. Dwight

Christmas Minstrelsy

The minstrels played their Christmas tune
To-night beneath my cottage eaves;
While smitten by a lofty moon,
The encircling laurels, thick with leaves,
Gave back a rich and dazzling sheen,
That overpowered their natural green.

Through hill and valley every breeze
Had sunk to rest with folded wings:
Keen was the air, but could not freeze
Nor check the music of the strings;
So stout and hardy were the band
That scraped the chords with strenuous hand.

And who but listened?—till was paid
Respect to every inmate's claim:
The greeting given, the music played,
In honor of each household name,
Duly pronounced with lusty call,
And a merry Christmas wished to all.

WILLIAM WORDSWORTH

Christmas Bells

I heard the bells on Christmas Day
Their old, familiar carols play,
And wild and sweet
The words repeat
Of peace on earth, good-will to men!

And thought how, as the day had come,
The belfries of all Christendom
Had rolled along
The unbroken song
Of peace on earth, good-will to men!

Till, ringing, singing on its way,
The world revolved from night to day,
A voice, a chime,
A chant sublime
Of peace on earth, good-will to men!

Then from each black, accursed mouth
The cannon thundered in the South,
And with the sound
The carols drowned
Of peace on earth, good-will to men!

It was as if an earthquake rent
The hearth-stones of a continent,

And made forlorn
The households born
Of peace on earth, good-will to men!

And in despair I bowed my head;
"There is no peace on earth," I said,
"For hate is strong,
And mocks the song
Of peace on earth, good-will to men!"

Then pealed the bells more loud and deep:
"God is not dead, nor doth He sleep!
The Wrong shall fail,
The Right prevail,
With peace on earth, good-will to men!"

HENRY WADSWORTH LONGFELLOW

from LOUISA MAY ALCOTT'S

Little Women

Chapter 1

PLAYING PILGRIMS

"Christmas won't be Christmas without any presents," grumbled Jo, lying on the rug.

"It's so dreadful to be poor!" sighed Meg, looking down at her old dress.

"I don't think it's fair for some girls to have plenty of pretty things, and other girls nothing at all," added little Amy, with an injured sniff.

"We've got Father and Mother and each other," said Beth, contentedly, from her corner.

The four young faces on which the firelight shone brightened at the cheerful words, but darkened again as Jo said sadly: "We haven't got Father, and shall not have him for a long time." She didn't say "perhaps never," but each silently added it, thinking of father far away, where the fighting was.

Nobody spoke for a minute; then Meg said in an altered tone: "You know the reason Mother proposed not having any presents this Christmas was because it is going to be a hard winter for everyone; and she thinks we ought not to spend money for pleasure when our men are suffering so in the army. We can't do much, but we can make our little sacrifices, and ought to do it gladly. But I am afraid I don't"; and Meg shook her head, and she thought regretfully of all the pretty things she wanted.

"But I don't think the little we should spend would do any good. We've each got a dollar, and the army wouldn't be much helped by our giving that. I agree not to expect anything from Mother or you, but I do want to buy *Undine and Sintram* for myself; I've wanted it *so* long," said Jo, who was a bookworm.

"I planned to spend mine on new music," said Beth, with a little sigh, which no one heard but the hearth-brush and kettle-holder.

"I shall get a nice box of Faber's drawing pencils; I really need them," said Amy, decidedly.

"Mother didn't say anything about our money, and she won't wish us to give up everything. Let's each buy what we want, and have a little fun; I'm sure we work hard enough to earn it," cried Jo, examining the heels of her shoes in a gentlemanly manner.

"I know *I* do—teaching those tiresome children nearly all day when I am longing to enjoy myself at home," began Meg, in the complaining tone again.

"You don't have half such a hard time as I do," said Jo. "How would you like to be shut up for hours with a nervous, fussy old lady, who keeps you trotting, is never satisfied, and worries you till you're ready to fly out of the window or cry?"

"It's naughty to fret; but I do think washing dishes and keeping things tidy is the worst work in the world. It makes me cross; and my hands get so stiff, I can't practise well at all"; and Beth looked at her rough hands with a sigh that anyone could hear that time.

"I don't believe any of you suffer as I do," cried Amy; "for you don't have to go to school with impertinent girls, who plague you if you don't know your lessons, and laugh at your dresses, and label your father if he isn't rich, and insult you when your nose isn't nice."

"If you mean *libel,* I'd say so, and not talk about *labels,* as if Papa was a pickle-bottle," advised Jo, laughing.

"I know what I mean, and you needn't be *statirical* about it. It's proper to use good words, and improve your *vocabulary,*" returned Amy, with dignity.

"Don't peck at one another, children. Don't you wish we had the money Papa lost when we were little, Jo? Dear me! how happy and good we'd be, if we had no worries!" said Meg, who could remember better times.

"You said, the other day, you thought we were a deal happier than the King children, for they were fighting and fretting all the time, in spite of their money."

"So I did, Beth. Well, I think we are; for, though we do have to work, we make fun for ourselves, and are a pretty jolly set, as Jo would say."

"Jo does use such slang words!" observed Amy, with a reproving look at the long figure stretched on the rug. Jo immediately sat up, put her hands in her pockets, and began to whistle.

"Don't, Jo; it's so boyish!"

"That's why I do it."

"I detest rude, unladylike girls!"

"I hate affected, niminy-piminy chits!"

" 'Birds in their little nests agree,' " sang Beth, the peace-maker, with such a funny face that both sharp voices softened to a laugh, and the "pecking" ended for that time.

"Really, girls, you are both to be blamed," said Meg, beginning to lecture in her elder-sisterly fashion. "You are old enough to leave off boyish tricks, and to behave better, Josephine. It didn't matter so much when you were a little girl; but now you are so tall, and turn up your hair, you should remember that you are a young lady."

"I'm not! and if turning up my hair makes me one, I'll wear it in two tails till I'm twenty," cried Jo, pulling off her net, and shaking down her chestnut mane. "I hate to think I've got to grow up, and be Miss March, and wear long gowns, and look as prim as a China-aster! It's bad enough to be a girl, anyway, when I like boys' games and work and manners! I can't get over my disappointment in not being a boy; and it's worse than ever now, for I'm dying to go and fight with Papa, and I can only stay at home and knit, like a poky old woman!" And Jo shook the blue army sock till the needles rattled like castanets, and her ball bounded across the room.

"Poor Jo! It's too bad, but it can't be helped; so you must try to be contented with making your name boyish, and playing brother to us girls," said Beth, stroking the rough head at her knee with a hand that all the dish-washing and dusting in the world could not make ungentle in its touch.

"As for you, Amy," continued Meg, "you are altogether too particular and prim. Your airs are funny now; but you'll grow up an affected little goose, if you don't take care. I like your nice manners and refined ways of speaking when you don't try to be elegant; but your absurd words are as bad as Jo's slang."

"If Jo is a tomboy and Amy a goose, what am I, please?" asked Beth, ready to share the lecture.

"You're a dear, and nothing else," answered Meg, warmly; and no one contradicted her, for the "Mouse" was the pet of the family.

As young readers like to know "how people look," we will take this moment to give them a little sketch of the four sisters, who sat knitting away in the twilight, while the December snow fell quietly without, and the fire crackled cheerfully within. It was a comfortable old room, though the carpet was faded and the furniture very plain; for a good picture or two hung on the walls, books filled the recesses, chrysanthemums and Christmas roses bloomed in the windows, and a pleasant atmosphere of home-peace pervaded it.

Margaret, the eldest of the four, was sixteen, and very pretty, being plump and fair, with large eyes, plenty of soft, brown hair, a sweet mouth, and white hands, of which she was rather vain. Fifteen-year-old Jo was very tall, thin, and brown, and reminded one of a colt; for she never seemed to know what to do with her long limbs, which were very much in her way. She had a decided mouth, a comical nose, and sharp, grey eyes, which appeared to see everything, and were by turns fierce, funny, or thoughtful. Her long, thick hair was her one beauty; but it was usually bundled in a net, to be out of her way. Round shoulders had Jo, big hands and feet, a fly-away look to her clothes, and the uncomfortable appearance of a girl who was rapidly shooting up into a woman, and didn't like it. Elizabeth—or Beth, as everyone called her—was a rosy, smooth-haired, bright-eyed girl of thirteen, with a shy manner, a timid voice, and a peaceful expression, which was seldom disturbed. Her father called her "Little Tranquillity," and the name suited her excellently; for she seemed to live in a happy world of her own, only venturing out to meet the few whom she trusted and loved. Amy, though the youngest, was a most important person—in her own opinion at least. A regular snow-maiden, with blue eyes, and yellow hair, curling on her shoulders, pale and slender, and always carrying herself like a young lady mindful of her manners. What the characters of the four sisters were we will leave to be found out.

The clock struck six; and, having swept up the hearth,

Beth put a pair of slippers down to warm. Somehow the sight of the old shoes had a good effect upon the girls; for mother was coming, and everyone brightened to welcome her. Meg stopped lecturing, and lighted the lamp, Amy got out of the easy-chair without being asked, and Jo forgot how tired she was as she sat up to hold the slippers nearer to the blaze.

"They are quite worn out; Marmee must have a new pair."

"I thought I'd get her some with my dollar," said Beth.

"No, I shall!" cried Amy.

"I'm the oldest," began Meg, but Jo cut in with a decided: "I'm the man of the family now Papa is away, and *I* shall provide the slippers, for he told me to take special care of Mother while he was gone."

"I'll tell you what we'll do," said Beth; "let's each get her something for Christmas, and not get anything for ourselves."

"That's like you, dear! What will we get?" exclaimed Jo.

Everyone thought soberly for a minute; then Meg announced as if the idea was suggested by the sight of her own pretty hands, "I shall give her a nice pair of gloves."

"Army shoes, best to be had," cried Jo.

"Some handkerchiefs, all hemmed," said Beth.

"I'll get a little bottle of cologne; she likes it, and it won't cost much, so I'll have some left to buy my pencils," added Amy.

"How will we give the things?" asked Meg.

"Put them on the table, and bring her in and see her

open the bundles. Don't you remember how we used to do on our birthdays?" answered Jo.

"I used to be *so* frightened when it was my turn to sit in the big chair with the crown on, and see you all come marching round to give the presents, with a kiss. I liked the things and the kisses, but it was dreadful to have you sit looking at me while I opened the bundles," said Beth, who was toasting her face and the bread for tea, at the same time.

"Let Marmee think we are getting things for ourselves, and then surprise her. We must go shopping tomorrow afternoon, Meg; there is so much to do about the play for Christmas night," said Jo, marching up and down, with her hands behind her back and her nose in the air.

"I don't mean to act any more after this time; I'm getting too old for such things," observed Meg, who was as much a child as ever about "dressing-up" frolics.

"You won't stop, I know, as long as you can trail round in a white gown with your hair down, and wear gold-paper jewellery. You are the best actress we've got, and there'll be an end of everything if you quit the boards," said Jo. "We ought to rehearse tonight. Come here, Amy, and do the fainting scene, for you are as stiff as a poker in that."

"I can't help it; I never saw anyone faint, and I don't choose to make myself all black and blue, tumbling flat as you do. If I can go down easily, I'll drop; if I can't, I shall fall into a chair and be graceful; I don't care if Hugo does come at me with a pistol," returned Amy, who was not gifted with dramatic power, but was chosen because she was small enough to be borne out shrieking by the villain of the piece.

"Do it this way; clasp your hands so, and stagger across the room, crying frantically, 'Roderigo! save me! save me!' " and away went Jo, with a melodramatic scream which was truly thrilling. Amy followed, but she poked her hands out stiffly before her, and jerked herself along as if she went by machinery; and her "Ow!" was more suggestive of pins being run into her than of fear and anguish. Jo gave a despairing groan, and Meg laughed outright, while Beth let her bread burn as she watched the fun with interest.

"It's no use! Do the best you can when the time comes, and if the audience laugh, don't blame me. Come on, Meg."

Then things went smoothly, for Don Pedro defied the world in a speech of two pages without a single break; Hagar, the witch, chanted an awful incantation over her kettleful of simmering toads, with weird effect; Roderigo rent his chains asunder manfully, and Hugo died in agonies of remorse and arsenic, with a wild "Ha! ha!"

"It's the best we've had yet," said Meg, as the dead villain sat up and rubbed his elbows.

"I don't see how you can write and act such splendid things, Jo. You're a regular Shakespeare!" exclaimed Beth, who firmly believed that her sisters were gifted with wonderful genius in all things.

"Not quite," replied Jo modestly. "I do think '*The Witch's Curse*, an Operatic Tragedy' is rather a nice thing; but I'd like to try *Macbeth*, if we only had a trap-door for Banquo. I always wanted to do the killing part. 'Is that a dagger I see before me?' " muttered Jo, rolling her eyes and clutching at the air, as she had seen a famous tragedian do.

"No, it's the toasting fork, with Mother's shoe on it instead of the bread. Beth's stage-struck!" cried Meg, and the rehearsal ended in a general burst of laughter.

"Glad to find you so merry, my girls," said a cheery voice at the door, and actors and audience turned to welcome a tall, motherly lady, with a "can-I-help-you" look about her which was truly delightful. She was not elegantly dressed, but a noble-looking woman, and the girls thought the grey cloak and unfashionable bonnet covered the most splendid mother in the world.

"Well, dearies, how have you got on today? There was so much to do, getting the boxes ready to go tomorrow, that I didn't come home to dinner. Has anyone called, Beth? How is your cold, Meg? Jo, you look tired to death. Come and kiss me, baby."

While making these maternal inquiries, Mrs. March got her wet things off, her warm slippers on, and sitting down in the easy-chair, drew Amy to her lap, preparing to enjoy the happiest hour of her busy day. The girls flew about, trying to make things comfortable, each in her own way. Meg arranged the tea-table; Jo brought wood and set chairs, dropping, overturning, and clattering everything she touched; Beth trotted to and fro between parlour and kitchen, quiet and busy; while Amy gave directions to everyone, as she sat with her hands folded.

As they gathered about the table, Mrs. March said, with a particularly happy face, "I've got a treat for you after supper."

A quick, bright smile went round like a streak of sunshine.

Beth clapped her hands, regardless of the biscuit she held, and Jo tossed up her napkin, crying, "A letter! A letter! Three cheers for Father!"

"Yes, a nice long letter. He is well, and thinks he shall get through the cold season better than we feared. He sends all sorts of loving wishes for Christmas, and an especial message to you girls," said Mrs. March, patting her pocket as if she had got a treasure there.

"Hurry and get done! Don't stop to quirk your little finger, and simper over your plate, Amy," cried Jo, choking in her tea, and dropping her bread, butter side down, on the carpet in her haste to get at the treat. Beth ate no more, but crept away, to sit in her shadowy corner and brood over the delight to come, till the others were ready.

"I think it was so splendid of Father to go as chaplain when he was too old to be drafted, and not strong enough for a soldier," said Meg, warmly.

"Don't I wish I could go as a drummer, a *vivan*—what's its name? or a nurse, so I could be near him and help him," exclaimed Jo, with a groan.

"It must be very disagreeable to sleep in a tent, and eat all sorts of bad-tasting things, and drink out of a tin mug," sighed Amy.

"When will he come home, Marmee?" asked Beth, with a little quiver in her voice.

"Not for many months, dear, unless he is sick. He will stay and do his work faithfully as long as he can, and we won't ask for him back a minute sooner than he can be spared. Now come and hear the letter."

They all drew to the fire, mother in the big chair, with Beth at her feet, Meg and Amy perched on either arm of the chair, and Jo leaning on the back, where no one would see any sign of emotion if the letter should happen to be touching. Very few letters were written in those hard times that were not touching, especially those which fathers sent home. In this one little was said of the hardships endured, the dangers faced, or the home-sickness conquered; it was a cheerful, hopeful letter, full of lively descriptions of camp life, marches, and military news; and only at the end did the writer's heart overflow with fatherly love and longing for the little girls at home.

"Give them all my dear love and a kiss. Tell them I think of them by day, pray for them by night, and find my best comfort in their affection at all times. A year seems very long to wait before I see them, but remind them that while we wait we may all work, so that these hard days need not be wasted. I know they will remember all I said to them, that they will be loving children to you, will do their duty faithfully, fight their bosom enemies bravely, and conquer themselves so beautifully, that when I come back to them I may be fonder and prouder than ever of my little women."

Everybody sniffed when they came to that part; Jo wasn't ashamed of the great tear that dropped off the end of her nose, and Amy never minded the rumpling of her curls as she hid her face on her mother's shoulder and sobbed out, "I *am* a selfish girl! but I'll truly try to be better, so he mayn't be disappointed in me by and by."

"We all will!" cried Meg. "I think too much of my looks, and hate to work, but won't any more, if I can help it."

"I'll try and be what he loves to call me, 'a little woman,' and not be rough and wild; but do my duty here instead of wanting to be somewhere else," said Jo, thinking that keeping her temper at home was a much harder task than facing a rebel or two down South.

Beth said nothing, but wiped away her tears with the blue army sock, and began to knit with all her might, losing no time in doing the duty that lay nearest her, while she resolved in her quiet little soul to be all that father hoped to find her when the year brought round the happy coming home.

Mrs. March broke the silence that followed Jo's words, by saying in her cheery voice, "Do you remember how you used to play *Pilgrim's Progress* when you were little things? Nothing delighted you more than to have me tie my piece-bags on your backs for burdens, give you hats and sticks and rolls of paper, and let you travel through the house from the cellar, which was the City of Destruction, up, up, to the housetop, where you had all the lovely things you could collect to make a Celestial City."

"What fun it was, especially going by the lions, fighting Apollyon, and passing through the Valley where the hobgoblins were!" said Jo.

"I liked the place where the bundles fell off and tumbled downstairs," said Meg.

"My favourite part was when we came out on the flat roof where our flowers and arbours and pretty things were, and all stood and sang for joy up there in the sunshine," said Beth, smiling, as if that pleasant moment had come back to her.

"I don't remember much about it, except that I was afraid

of the cellar and the dark entry, and always liked the cake and milk we had up at the top. If I wasn't too old for such things, I'd rather like to play it over again," said Amy, who began to talk of renouncing childish things at the mature age of twelve.

"We never are too old for this, my dear, because it is a play we are playing all the time in one way or another. Our burdens are here, our road is before us, and the longing for goodness and happiness is the guide that leads us through many troubles and mistakes to the peace which is a true Celestial City. Now, my little pilgrims, suppose you begin again, not in play, but in earnest, and see how far on you can get before Father comes home."

"Really, Mother? Where are our bundles?" asked Amy, who was a very literal young lady.

"Each of you told what your burden was just now, except Beth; I rather think she hasn't got any," said her mother.

"Yes, I have; mine is dishes and dusters, and envying girls with nice pianos, and being afraid of people."

Beth's bundle was such a funny one that everybody wanted to laugh; but nobody did, for it would have hurt her feelings very much.

"Let us do it," said Meg, thoughtfully. "It is only another name for trying to be good, and the story may help us; for though we do want to be good, it's hard work, and we forget, and don't do our best."

"We were in the Slough of Despond tonight, and Mother came and pulled us out as Help did in the book. We ought to have our roll of directions, like Christian. What shall we do about that?" asked Jo, delighted with the fancy which lent a little romance to the very dull task of doing her duty.

"Look under your pillows, Christmas morning, and you will find your guide-book," replied Mrs. March.

They talked over the new plan while old Hannah cleared the table; then out came the four little work-baskets, and the needles flew as the girls made sheets for Aunt March. It was uninteresting sewing, but tonight no one grumbled. They adopted Jo's plan of dividing the long seams into four parts, and calling the quarters Europe, Asia, Africa, and America, and in that way got on capitally, especially when they talked about the different countries, as they stitched their way through them.

At nine they stopped work, and sang, as usual, before they went to bed.

No one but Beth could get much music out of the old piano; but she had a way of softly touching the yellow keys, and making a pleasant accompaniment to the simple songs they sang. Meg had a voice like a flute, and she and her mother led the little choir. Amy chirped like a cricket, and Jo wandered through the airs at her own sweet will, always coming out at the wrong place with a croak or a quaver that spoilt the most pensive tune. They had always done this from the time they could lisp:

"Crinkle, crinkle, 'ittle 'tar."

and it had become a household custom, for the mother was a born singer. The first sound in the morning was her voice, as she went about the house singing like a lark; and the last sound at night was the same cheery sound, for the girls never grew too old for that familiar lullaby.

Chapter 2

A MERRY CHRISTMAS

Jo was the first to wake in the grey dawn of Christmas morning. No stockings hung at the fireplace, and for a moment she felt as much disappointed as she did long ago, when her little sock fell down because it was so crammed with goodies. Then she remembered her mother's promise, and, slipping her hand under her pillow, drew out a little crimson-covered book. She knew it very well, for it was that beautiful old story of the best life ever lived, and Jo felt that it was a true guide-book for any pilgrim going the long journey. She woke Meg with a "Merry Christmas," and bade her see what was under her pillow. A green-covered book appeared, with the same picture inside, and a few words written by their mother, which made their one present very precious in their eyes. Presently Beth and Amy woke, to rummage and find their little books also—one, dove-coloured, the other blue; and all sat looking at and talking about them, while the east grew rosy with the coming day.

In spite of her small vanities, Margaret had a sweet and pious nature, which unconsciously influenced her sisters, especially Jo, who loved her very tenderly, and obeyed her because her advice was so gently given.

"Girls," said Meg seriously, looking from the tumbled head beside her to the two little night-capped ones in the room beyond, "Mother wants us to read and love and mind these books, and we must begin at once. We used to be faithful about it; but since Father went away, and all this war trouble unsettled us, we have neglected many things. You can do as you please; but *I* shall keep my book on the table here, and read a little every morning as soon as I wake, for I know it will do me good, and help me through the day."

Then she opened her new book and began to read. Jo put her arm around her, and leaning cheek to cheek, read also, with the quiet expression so seldom seen on her restless face.

"How good Meg is! Come, Amy, let's do as they do. I'll help you with the hard words, and they'll explain things if we don't understand," whispered Beth, very much impressed by the pretty books and her sisters' example. "I'm glad mine is blue," said Amy; and then the rooms were very still while the pages were softly turned, and the winter sunshine crept in to touch the bright heads and serious faces with a Christmas greeting.

"Where is Mother?" asked Meg, as she and Jo ran down to thank her for their gifts, half an hour later. "Goodness only knows. Some poor creeter come a'beggin', and your ma went straight off to see what was needed. There never *was* such a woman for givin' away vittles and drink, clothes, and firin'," replied Hannah, who had lived with the family since

Meg was born, and was considered by them all more as a friend than a servant.

"She will be back soon, I think; so fry your cake, and have everything ready," said Meg, looking over the presents which were collected in a basket and kept under the sofa, ready to be produced at the proper time. "Why, where is Amy's bottle of cologne?" she added, as the little flask did not appear. "She took it out a minute ago, and went off with it to put a ribbon on it, or some such notion," replied Jo, dancing about the room to take the first stiffness off the new army-slippers.

"How nice my handkerchiefs look, don't they! Hannah washed, and ironed them for me, and I marked them all myself," said Beth, looking proudly at the somewhat uneven letters which had cost her such labour.

"Bless the child! she's gone and put 'Mother' on them instead of 'M. March.' How funny!" cried Jo, taking up one.

"Isn't it right? I thought it was better to do it so, because Meg's initials are 'M. M.,' and I don't want anyone to use these but Marmee," said Beth, looking troubled.

"It's all right, dear, and a very pretty idea—quite sensible, too, for no one can ever mistake them now. It will please her very much, I know," said Meg, with a frown for Jo and a smile for Beth.

"There's Mother. Hide the basket, quick!" cried Jo, as a door slammed, and steps sounded in the hall.

Amy came in hastily, and looked rather abashed when she saw her sisters all waiting for her.

"Where have you been, and what are you hiding behind

you?" asked Meg, surprised to see, by her hood and cloak, that Lazy Amy had been out so early.

"Don't laugh at me, Jo! I didn't mean anyone should know till the time came. I only meant to change the little bottle for a big one, and I gave *all* my money to get it, and I'm truly trying not to be selfish any more."

As she spoke, Amy showed the handsome flask which replaced the cheap one; and looked so earnest and humble in her little effort to forget herself that Meg hugged her on the spot, and Jo pronounced her "a trump," while Beth ran to the window and picked her finest rose to ornament the stately bottle.

"You see, I felt ashamed of my present, after reading and talking about being good this morning, so I ran round the corner and changed it the minute I was up; and I'm *so* glad, for mine is the handsomest now."

Another bang of the street door sent the basket under the sofa, and the girls to the table, eager for breakfast.

"Merry Christmas, Marmee! Many of them! Thank you for our books; we read some, and mean to, every day," they cried, in chorus.

"Merry Christmas, little daughters! I'm glad you began at once, and hope you will keep on. But I want to say one word before we sit down. Not far away from here lies a poor woman with a little new-born baby. Six children are huddled into one bed to keep from freezing, for they have no fire. There is nothing to eat over there; and the oldest boy came to tell me they were suffering hunger and cold. My girls, will you give them your breakfast as a Christmas present?"

They were all unusually hungry, having waited nearly an hour, and for a minute no one spoke; only a minute, for Jo exclaimed impetuously: "I'm so glad you came before we began!"

"May I go and help carry the things to the poor little children?" said Beth, eagerly.

"*I* shall take the cream and the muffins," added Amy, heroically, giving up the articles she most liked.

Meg was already covering the buckwheats, and piling the bread into one big plate.

"I thought you'd do it," said Mrs. March, smiling as if satisfied. "You shall all go and help me, and when we come back we will have bread and milk for breakfast, and make it up at dinner-time."

They were soon ready, and the procession set out. Fortunately it was early, and they went through back streets, so few people saw them, and no one laughed at the queer party.

A poor, bare, miserable room it was, with broken windows, no fire, ragged bed-clothes, a sick mother, wailing baby, and a group of pale, hungry children cuddled under one old quilt, trying to keep warm.

How the big eyes stared and blue lips smiled as the girls went in!

"*Ach, mein Gott!* it is good angels come to us!" said the poor woman, crying for joy.

"Funny angels in hoods and mittens," said Jo and set them laughing.

In a few minutes it really did seem as if kind spirits had been at work there. Hannah, who had carried wood, made a fire, and stopped up the broken panes with old hats and her own cloak. Mrs. March gave the mother tea and gruel, and comforted her with promises of help, while she dressed the little baby as tenderly as if it had been her own. The girls, meantime, spread the table, set the children round the fire, and fed them like so many hungry birds—laughing, talking, and trying to understand the funny broken English.

"Das ist gut!" "Die Engelkinder!" cried the poor things, as they ate, and warmed their purple hands at the comfortable blaze.

The girls had never been called angel children before, and thought it very agreeable, especially Jo, who had been considered a "Sancho" ever since she was born. That was a very happy breakfast, though they didn't get any of it; and when they went away, leaving comfort behind, I think there were not in all the city four merrier people than the hungry little girls who gave away their breakfasts and contented themselves with bread and milk on Christmas morning.

"That's loving our neighbour better than ourselves, and I like it," said Meg, as they set out their presents, while their mother was upstairs collecting clothes for the poor Hummels.

Not a very splendid show, but there was a great deal of love done up in the few little bundles; and the tall vase of red roses, white chrysanthemums, and trailing vines, which stood in the middle, gave quite an elegant air to the table.

"She's coming! Strike up, Beth! Open the door, Amy! Three cheers for Marmee!" cried Jo, prancing about, while Meg went to conduct Mother to the seat of honour.

Beth played her gayest march, Amy threw open the door,

and Meg enacted escort with great dignity. Mrs. March was both surprised and touched; and smiled with her eyes full as she examined her presents, and read the little notes which accompanied them. The slippers went on at once, a new handkerchief was slipped into her pocket, well scented with Amy's cologne, the rose was fastened in her bosom, and the nice gloves were pronounced a "perfect fit."

There was a good deal of laughing and kissing and explaining, in the simple, loving fashion which makes these home festivals so pleasant at the time, so sweet to remember long afterwards, and then all fell to work.

The morning charities and ceremonies took so much time that the rest of the day was devoted to preparations for the evening festivities.

Not rich enough to afford any great outlay for private performances, the girls put their wits to work, and—necessity being the mother of invention—made whatever they needed. Very clever were some of their productions—pasteboard guitars, antique lamps made of old-fashioned butter-boats covered with silver paper, gorgeous robes of old cotton glittering with tin spangle from a pickle factory, and armour covered with the same useful diamond-shaped bits, left in the sheets when the lids of tin preserve-pots were cut out. The furniture was used to being turned topsy-turvy, and the big chamber was the scene of many innocent revels.

No gentlemen were admitted; so Jo played male parts to her heart's content, and took immense satisfaction in a pair of russet-leather boots given her by a friend. These boots, an old foil, and a slashed doublet once used by an artist for some picture, were Jo's chief treasures, and appeared on all occasions. The smallness of the company made it necessary for the two principal actors to take several parts apiece; and they certainly deserved some credit for the hard work they did in learning three or four different parts, whisking in and out of various costumes, and managing the stage besides. It was excellent drill for their memories, a harmless amusement, and employed many hours which otherwise would have been idle, lonely, or spent in less profitable society.

On Christmas night, a dozen girls piled on to the bed, which was the dress-circle, and sat before the blue and yellow chintz curtains in a most flattering state of expectancy. There was a good deal of rustling and whispering behind the curtain, a trifle of lamp-smoke, and an occasional giggle from Amy, who was apt to get hysterical in the excitement of the moment. Presently a bell sounded, the curtains flew apart, and the Operatic Tragedy began.

"A gloomy wood," according to the one play-bill, was represented by a few shrubs in pots, green baize on the floor, and a cave in the distance. This cave was made with a clothes-horse for a roof, bureaus for walls; and in it was a small furnace in full blast, with a black spot on it, and an old witch bending over it. The stage was dark, and the glow of the furnace had a fine effect, especially as real steam issued from the kettle when the witch took off the cover. A moment was allowed for the first thrill to subside; then Hugo, the villain, stalked in with clanking sword at his side, a slouched hat, black beard, mysterious cloak, and the boots. After pacing to and fro in much agitation, he struck his forehead, and burst out in a wild strain, singing of his hatred to Roderigo, his love for Zara, and his pleasing resolution to kill the one and win the other. The gruff tones of Hugo's voice, with an occasional shout when his feelings overcame him, were very impressive, and the audience applauded the moment he paused for breath. Bowing with the air of one accustomed to public praise, he stole to the cavern, and ordered Hagar to come forth with a commanding "What ho, minion! I need thee!"

Out came Meg, with grey horse-hair hanging about her face, a red and black robe, a staff, and cabbalistic signs upon her cloak. Hugo demanded a potion to make Zara adore him, and one to destroy Roderigo. Hagar, in a fine dramatic melody, promised both, and proceeded to call up the spirit who would bring the love philtre:

"Hither, hither, from my home,
Airy sprite, I bid thee come!
Born of roses, fed on dew,
Charms and potions canst thou brew?"

"Bring me here, with elfin speed,
The fragrant philtre which I need;
Make it sweet and swift and strong,
Spirit, answer now my song!"

A soft strain of music sounded, and then at the back of the cave appeared a little figure in cloudy white, with glittering wings, golden hair, and a garland of roses on its head. Waving a wand, it sang:

"Hither I come,
From my airy home,
Afar in the silver moon.
Take this magic spell,
And use it well,
Or its power will vanish soon!"

And, dropping a small, gilded bottle at the witch's feet, the spirit vanished. Another chant from Hagar produced another apparition—not a lovely one; for, with a bang, an ugly black imp appeared, and, having croaked a reply, tossed a dark bottle at Hugo, and disappeared with a mocking laugh. Having warbled his thanks and put the potions in his boots, Hugo departed; and Hagar informed the audience that, as he had killed a few of her friends in times past, she has cursed him, and intends to thwart his plans, and be revenged on him. Then the curtain fell, and the audience reposed and ate candy while discussing the merits of the play.

A good deal of hammering went on before the curtain rose again; but when it became evident what a masterpiece of stage-carpentering had been got up, no one murmured at the delay. It was truly superb! A tower rose to the ceiling; half-way up appeared a window, with a lamp burning at it, and behind the white curtain appeared Zara in a lovely blue and silver dress, waiting for Roderigo. He came in gorgeous array, with plumed cap, red cloak, chestnut love-locks, a guitar, and the boots, of course. Kneeling at the foot of the tower, he sang a serenade in melting tones. Zara replied, and, after a musical dialogue, consented to fly. Then came the grand effect of the play. Roderigo produced a rope ladder, with five steps to it, threw up one end, and invited Zara to descend. Timidly she crept from her lattice, put her hand on Roderigo's shoulder, and was about to leap gracefully down, when, "Alas! alas for Zara!" she forgot her train—it caught in the window, the tower tottered, leant forward, fell with a crash, and buried the unhappy lovers in the ruins!

A universal shriek arose as the russet boots waved wildly from the wreck, and a golden head emerged, exclaiming, "I told you so! I told you so!" With wonderful presence of mind, Don Pedro, the cruel sire, rushed in, dragged out his daughter, with a hasty aside: "Don't laugh! Act as if it was all right!"—and, ordering Roderigo up, banished him from the kingdom with wrath and scorn. Though decidedly shaken by the fall of the tower upon him, Roderigo defied the old gentleman, and refused to stir. This dauntless example fired Zara: she also defied her sire, and he ordered them both to the deepest dungeons of the castle. A stout little retainer came in with chains, and led them away, looking very much frightened, and evidently forgetting the speech he ought to have made.

Act third was the castle hall; and here Hagar appeared, having come to free the lovers and finish Hugo. She hears him coming, and hides; sees him put the potions into two cups of wine, and bid the timid little servant: "Bear them to the captives in their cells, and tell them I shall come anon." The servant takes Hugo aside to tell him something, and Hagar changes the cups for two others which are harmless. Ferdinando, the "minion," carries them away, and Hagar puts back the cup which holds the poison meant for Roderigo. Hugo, getting thirsty after a long warble, drinks it, loses his wits, and, after a good deal of clutching and stamping, falls flat and dies; while Hagar informs him what she has done in a song of exquisite power and melody.

This was a truly thrilling scene, though some persons might have thought that the sudden tumbling down of a quantity of long hair rather marred the effect of the villain's death. He was called before the curtain, and with great propriety appeared, leading Hagar, whose singing was considered more wonderful than all the rest of the performance put together.

Act fourth displayed the despairing Roderigo on the point of stabbing himself, because he has been told that Zara has deserted him. Just as the dagger is at his heart, a lovely song is sung under his window, informing him that Zara is true, but in danger, and he can save her, if he will. A key is thrown in, which unlocks the door, and in a spasm of rapture he tears off his chains, and rushes away to find and rescue his lady-love.

Act fifth opened with a stormy scene between Zara and Don Pedro. He wishes her to go into a convent, but she won't hear of it; and, after a touching appeal, is about to faint, when Roderigo dashes in and demands her hand. Don Pedro refuses, because he is not rich. They shout and gesticulate tremendously, but cannot agree, and Roderigo is about to bear away the exhausted Zara, when the timid servant enters with a letter and a bag from Hagar, who has mysteriously disappeared. The letter informs the party that she bequeaths untold wealth to the young pair, and an awful doom to Don Pedro, if he doesn't make them happy. The bag is opened, and several quarts of tin money shower down upon the stage, till it is quite glorified with the glitter. This entirely softens the "stern sire": he consents without a murmur, all join in a joyful chorus, and the curtain falls upon the lovers kneeling to receive Don Pedro's blessing in attitudes of the most romantic grace.

Tumultuous applause followed, but received an unexpected check; for the cot-bed, on which the "dress-circle" was built, suddenly shut up, and extinguished the enthusiastic audience. Roderigo and Don Pedro flew to the rescue, and all were taken out unhurt, though many were speechless with laughter. The excitement had hardly subsided, when Hannah appeared, with "Mrs. March's compliments, and would the ladies walk down to supper."

This was a surprise, even to the actors; and, when they saw the table, they looked at one another in rapturous amazement. It was like Marmee to get up a little treat for them; but anything so fine as this was unheard of since the departed days of plenty. There was ice-cream—actually two dishes of it, pink and white—and cake and fruit and distracting French bonbons, and, in the middle of the table, four great bouquets of hot-house flowers.

It quite took their breath away; and they stared first at

the table and then at their mother, who looked as if she enjoyed it immensely.

"Is it fairies?" asked Amy.

"It's Santa Claus," said Beth.

"Mother did it,"; and Meg smiled her sweetest, in spite of her grey beard and white eyebrows.

"Aunt March had a good fit, and sent the supper," cried Jo, with a sudden inspiration.

"All wrong. Old Mr. Laurence sent it," replied Mrs. March.

"The Laurence boy's grandfather! What in the world put such a thing into his head? We don't know him!" exclaimed Meg.

"Hannah told one of his servants about your breakfast party. He is an odd old gentleman, but that pleased him. He knew my father, years ago; and he sent me a polite note this afternoon, saying he hoped I would allow him to express his friendly feeling towards my children by sending them a few trifles in honour of the day. I could not refuse; and so you have a little feast at night to make up for the bread-and-milk breakfast."

"That boy put it into his head, I know he did! He's a capital fellow, and I wish we could get acquainted. He looks as if he'd like to know us; but he's bashful, and Meg is so prim she won't let me speak to him when we pass," said Jo, as the plates went round, and the ice began to melt out of sight, with "Ohs!" and "Ahs!" of satisfaction.

"You mean the people who live in the big house next

door, don't you?" asked one of the girls. "My mother knows old Mr. Laurence; but says he's very proud, and doesn't like to mix with his neighbours. He keeps his grandson shut up, when he isn't riding or walking with his tutor, and makes him study very hard. We invited him to our party, but he didn't come. Mother says he's very nice, though he never speaks to us girls."

"Our cat ran away once, and he brought her back, and we talked over the fence, and we were getting on capitally—all about cricket, and so on—when he saw Meg coming, and walked off. I mean to know him some day; for he needs fun, I'm sure he does," said Jo decidedly.

"I like his manners, and he looks like a little gentleman; so I've no objection to your knowing him, if a proper opportunity comes. He brought the flowers himself; and I should have asked him in, if I had been sure what was going on upstairs. He looked so wistful as he went away, hearing the frolic, and evidently having none of his own."

"It's a mercy you didn't, Mother!" laughed Jo, looking at her boots. "But we'll have another play, some time, that he *can* see. Perhaps he'll help act; wouldn't that be jolly?"

"I never had such a fine bouquet before! How pretty it is!" And Meg examined her flowers with great interest.

"They *are* lovely. But Beth's roses are sweeter to me," said Mrs. March, smelling the half-dead posy in her belt.

Beth nestled up to her, and whispered softly, "I wish I could send my bunch to Father. I'm afraid he isn't having such a merry Christmas as we are."

Christmas Morning

If Bethlehem were here today
Or this were very long ago,
There wouldn't be a winter time
Nor any cold or snow.

I'd run out through the garden gate,
And down along the pasture walk;
And off beside the cattle barns
I'd hear a kind of gentle talk.

I'd move the heavy iron chain
And pull away the wooden pin;
I'd push the door a little bit
And tiptoe very softly in.

The pigeons and the yellow hens
And all the cows would stand away;
Their eyes would open wide to see
A lady in the manger hay,
If this were very long ago
And Bethlehem were here today.

And Mother held my hand and smiled—
I mean the lady would—and she
Would take the woolly blankets off
Her little boy so I could see.

His shut-up eyes would be asleep,
And he would look just like our John,
And he would be all crumpled too,
And have a pinkish color on.

I'd watch his breath go in and out,
His little clothes would be all white,
I'd slip my finger in his hand
To feel how he could hold it tight.

And she would smile and say, "Take care,"
The Mother, Mary, would, "Take care";
And I would kiss his little hand
And touch his hair.

While Mary put the blankets back
The gentle talk would soon begin,
And when I'd tiptoe softly out
I'd meet the wise men going in.

ELIZABETH MADOX ROBERTS

Deck the Halls

Deck the halls with boughs of holly.
Fa la la la la, la la la la.
'Tis the season to be jolly.
Fa la la la la, la la la la.
Don we now our gay apparel.
Fa la la, la la la, la la la.
Troll the ancient Yuletide carol:
Fa la la la la, la la la la.

See the blazing Yule before us.
Fa la la la la, la la la la.
Strike the harp and join the chorus.
Fa la la la la, la la la la.
Follow me in merry measure—
Fa la la, la la la, la la la—
While I tell of Yuletide treasure.
Fa la la la la, la la la la.

Fast away the old year passes.
Fa la la la la, la la la la.
Hail the new, ye lads and lasses.
Fa la la la la, la la la la.
Sing we joyous, all together—
Fa la la, la la la, la la la—
Heedless of the wind and weather.
Fa la la la la, la la la la.

TRADITIONAL CAROL

from GEORGE WITHER'S

A Christmas Carol

So now is come our joyful'st feast;
Let every man be jolly.
Each room with ivy leaves is dress'd,
And every post with holly.
Though some churls at our mirth repine,
Round your foreheads garlands twine,
Drown sorrow in a cup of wine,
And let us all be merry.

Now all our neighbors' chimneys smoke,
And Christmas blocks are burning;
Their ovens they with baked meats choke,

And all their spits are turning.
Without the door let sorrow lie,
And if for cold it hap to die,
We'll bury it in a Christmas pie,
And evermore be merry.

The Mistletoe

'Neath mistletoe, should chance arise,
You may be happy if you're wise.
Though bored you lie with pantomime
And Christmas fare and Christmas rhyme—
One fine old custom don't despise.

If you're a man of enterprise,
You'll find, I venture to surmise,
'Tis pleasant then at Christmas time
'Neath mistletoe!

You see they scarcely can disguise
The sparkle of their pretty eyes;
And no one thinks it is a crime,
When goes the merry Christmas chime,
A rare old rite to exercise
'Neath mistletoe!

J. ASHBY STERRY

Gloucestershire Wassailers' Song

Wassail! wassail! all over the town,
Our toast it is white, and our ale it is brown;
Our bowl is made of a maplin tree;
We be good fellows all;—I drink to thee.

Here's to our horse, and to his right ear,
God send our master a happy new year;
A happy new year as e'er he did see,—
With my wassailing bowl I drink to thee.

Here's to our mare, and to her right eye,
God send our mistress a good Christmas pie;
A good Christmas pie as e'er I did see,—
With my wassailing bowl I drink to thee.

Here's to our cow, and to her long tail,
God send our master us never may fail
Of a cup of good beer: I pray you draw near,
And our jolly wassail it's then you shall hear.

Be here any maids? I suppose here be some;
Sure they will not let young men stand on the cold stone!
Sing hey O, maids! come trole back the pin,
And the fairest maid in the house let us all in.

Come, butler, come, bring us a bowl of the best;
I hope your soul in heaven will rest;
But if you do bring us a bowl of the small,
Then down fall butler, and bowl and all.

OLD ENGLISH BALLAD

from CHARLES DICKENS'S

A Christmas Carol

Stave I

MARLEY'S GHOST

Marley was dead, to begin with. There is no doubt whatever about that. The register of his burial was signed by the clergyman, the clerk, the undertaker, and the chief mourner. Scrooge signed it. And Scrooge's name was good upon 'Change, for anything he chose to put his hand to.

Old Marley was as dead as a door-nail.

Mind! I don't mean to say that I know, of my own knowledge, what there is particularly dead about a door-nail. I might have been inclined, myself, to regard a coffin-nail as the deadest piece of ironmongery in the trade. But the wisdom of our ancestors is in the simile; and my unhallowed hands shall not disturb it, or the Country's done for. You will therefore permit me to repeat, emphatically, that Marley was as dead as a door-nail.

Scrooge knew he was dead? Of course he did. How could it be otherwise? Scrooge and he were partners for I don't know how many years. Scrooge was his sole executor, his sole administrator, his sole assign, his sole residuary legatee, his sole friend, and sole mourner. And even Scrooge was not so dreadfully cut up by the sad event, but that he was an excellent man of business on the very day of the funeral, and solemnised it with an undoubted bargain.

The mention of Marley's funeral brings me back to the point I started from. There is no doubt that Marley was dead. This must be distinctly understood, or nothing wonderful can come of the story I am going to relate. If we were not perfectly convinced that Hamlet's Father died before the play began, there would be nothing more remarkable in his taking a stroll at night, in an easterly wind, upon his own ramparts, than there would be in any other middle-aged gentleman rashly turning out after dark in a breezy spot—say Saint Paul's Churchyard for instance—literally to astonish his son's weak mind.

Scrooge never painted out Old Marley's name. There it stood, years afterwards, above the warehouse door: Scrooge and Marley. The firm was known as Scrooge and Marley. Sometimes people new to the business called Scrooge Scrooge, and sometimes Marley, but he answered to both names. It was all the same to him.

Oh! But he was a tight-fisted hand at the grindstone,

Scrooge! a squeezing, wrenching, grasping, scraping, clutching, covetous, old sinner! Hard and sharp as flint, from which no steel had ever struck out generous fire; secret, and self-contained, and solitary as an oyster. The cold within him froze his old features, nipped his pointed nose, shrivelled his cheek, stiffened his gait; made his eyes red, his thin lips blue; and spoke out shrewdly in his grating voice. A frosty rime was on his head, and on his eyebrows, and his wiry chin. He carried his own low temperature always about with him; he iced his office in the dog-days; and didn't thaw it one degree at Christmas.

External heat and cold had little influence on Scrooge. No warmth could warm, no wintry weather chill him. No wind that blew was bitterer than he, no falling snow was more intent upon its purpose, no pelting rain less open to entreaty. Foul weather didn't know where to have him. The heaviest rain, and snow, and hail, and sleet, could boast of the advantage over him in only one respect. They often "came down" handsomely, and Scrooge never did.

Nobody ever stopped him in the street to say, with gladsome looks, "My dear Scrooge, how are you? When will you come to see me?" No beggars implored him to bestow a trifle, no children asked him what it was o'clock, no man or woman ever once in all his life inquired the way to such and such a place, of Scrooge. Even the blind men's dogs appeared to know him; and when they saw him coming on, would tug their owners into doorways and up courts; and then would wag their tails as though they said, "No eye at all is better than an evil eye, dark master!"

But what did Scrooge care! It was the very thing he liked. To edge his way along the crowded paths of life, warning all human sympathy to keep its distance, was what the knowing ones call "nuts" to Scrooge.

Once upon a time—of all the good days in the year, on Christmas Eve—old Scrooge sat busy in his counting-house. It was cold, bleak, biting weather: foggy withal: and he could hear the people in the court outside, go wheezing up and down, beating their hands upon their breasts, and stamping their feet upon the pavement stones to warm them. The city clocks had only just gone three, but it was quite dark already—it had not been light all day—and candles were flaring in the windows of the neighbouring offices, like ruddy smears upon the palpable brown air. The fog came pouring in at every chink and keyhole, and was so dense without, that although the court was of the narrowest, the houses opposite were mere phantoms. To see the dingy cloud come drooping down, obscuring everything, one might have thought that Nature lived hard by, and was brewing on a large scale.

The door of Scrooge's counting-house was open that he might keep his eye upon his clerk, who in a dismal little cell beyond, a sort of tank, was copying letters. Scrooge had a very small fire, but the clerk's fire was so very much smaller that it looked like one coal. But he couldn't replenish it, for Scrooge kept the coal-box in his own room; and so surely as the clerk came in with the shovel, the master predicted that it would be necessary for them to part. Wherefore the clerk put on his white comforter, and tried to warm himself at the candle; in which effort, not being a man of a strong imagination, he failed.

"A merry Christmas, uncle! God save you!" cried a cheerful voice. It was the voice of Scrooge's nephew, who came upon him so quickly that this was the first intimation he had of his approach.

"Bah!" said Scrooge, "Humbug!"

He had so heated himself with rapid walking in the fog and frost, this nephew of Scrooge's, that he was all in a glow; his face was ruddy and handsome; his eyes sparkled, and his breath smoked again.

"Christmas a humbug, uncle!" said Scrooge's nephew. "You don't mean that, I am sure?"

"I do," said Scrooge. "Merry Christmas! What right have you to be merry? What reason have you to be merry? You're poor enough."

"Come, then," returned the nephew gaily. "What right have you to be dismal? What reason have you to be morose? You're rich enough."

Scrooge having no better answer ready on the spur of the moment, said, "Bah!" again; and followed it up with, "Humbug."

"Don't be cross, uncle!" said the nephew.

"What else can I be," returned the uncle, "when I live in such a world of fools as this? Merry Christmas! Out upon Merry Christmas! What's Christmas time to you but a time for paying bills without money; a time for finding yourself a year older, but not an hour richer; a time for balancing your books and having every item in 'em through a round dozen of months presented dead against you? If I could work my will," said Scrooge indignantly, "every idiot who goes about with 'Merry Christmas' on his lips, should be boiled with his own pudding, and buried with a stake of holly through his heart. He should!"

"Uncle!" pleaded the nephew.

"Nephew!" returned the uncle, sternly, "keep Christmas in your own way, and let me keep it in mine."

"Keep it!" repeated Scrooge's nephew. "But you don't keep it."

"Let me leave it alone, then," said Scrooge. "Much good may it do you! Much good it has ever done you!"

"There are many things from which I might have derived good, by which I have not profited, I dare say," returned the nephew. "Christmas among the rest. But I am sure I have always thought of Christmas time, when it has come round—apart from the veneration due to its sacred name and origin, if anything belonging to it can be apart from that—as a good time; a kind, forgiving, charitable, pleasant time; the only time I know of, in the long calendar of the year, when men and women seem by one consent to open their shut-up hearts freely, and to think of people below them as if they really were fellow-passengers to the grave, and not another race of creatures bound on other journeys. And therefore, uncle, though it has never put a scrap of gold or silver in my pocket, I believe that it *has* done me good, and *will* do me good; and I say, God bless it!"

The clerk in the tank involuntarily applauded. Becoming

immediately sensible of the impropriety, he poked the fire, and extinguished the last frail spark for ever.

"Let me hear another sound from *you*," said Scrooge, "and you'll keep your Christmas by losing your situation! You're quite a powerful speaker, sir," he added, turning to his nephew. "I wonder you don't go into Parliament."

"Don't be angry, uncle. Come! Dine with us to-morrow."

Scrooge said that he would see him—yes, indeed he did. He went the whole length of the expression, and said that he would see him in that extremity first.

"But why?" cried Scrooge's nephew. "Why?"

"Why did you get married?" said Scrooge.

"Because I fell in love."

"Because you fell in love!" growled Scrooge, as if that were the only one thing in the world more ridiculous than a merry Christmas. "Good afternoon!"

"Nay, uncle, but you never came to see me before that happened. Why give it as a reason for not coming now?"

"Good afternoon," said Scrooge.

"I want nothing from you; I ask nothing of you; why cannot we be friends?"

"Good afternoon," said Scrooge.

"I am sorry, with all my heart, to find you so resolute. We have never had any quarrel, to which I have been a party. But I have made the trial in homage to Christmas, and I'll keep my Christmas humour to the last. So A Merry Christmas, uncle!"

"Good afternoon!" said Scrooge.

"And A Happy New Year!"

"Good afternoon!" said Scrooge.

His nephew left the room without an angry word, notwithstanding. He stopped at the outer door to bestow the greetings of the season on the clerk, who, cold as he was, was warmer than Scrooge; for he returned them cordially.

"There's another fellow," muttered Scrooge; who overheard him, "my clerk, with fifteen shillings a week, and a wife and family, talking about a merry Christmas. I'll retire to Bedlam."

This lunatic, in letting Scrooge's nephew out, had let two other people in. They were portly gentlemen, pleasant to behold, and now stood, with their hats off, in Scrooge's office. They had books and papers in their hands, and bowed to him.

"Scrooge and Marley's, I believe," said one of the gentlemen, referring to his list. "Have I the pleasure of addressing Mr. Scrooge, or Mr. Marley?"

"Mr. Marley has been dead these seven years," Scrooge replied. "He died seven years ago, this very night."

"We have no doubt his liberality is well represented by his surviving partner," said the gentleman, presenting his credentials.

It certainly was; for they had been two kindred spirits. At the ominous word "liberality," Scrooge frowned, and shook his head, and handed the credentials back.

"At this festive season of the year, Mr. Scrooge," said the gentleman, taking up a pen, "it is more than usually desirable that we should make some slight provision for the Poor and destitute, who suffer greatly at the present time.

Many thousands are in want of common necessaries; hundreds of thousands are in want of common comforts, sir."

"Are there no prisons?" asked Scrooge.

"Plenty of prisons," said the gentleman, laying down the pen again.

"And the Union workhouses?" demanded Scrooge. "Are they still in operation?"

"They are. Still," returned the gentleman, "I wish I could say they were not."

"The Treadmill and the Poor Law are in full vigour, then?" said Scrooge.

"Both very busy, sir."

"Oh! I was afraid, from what you said at first, that something had occurred to stop them in their useful course," said Scrooge. "I'm very glad to hear it."

"Under the impression that they scarcely furnish Christian cheer of mind or body to the multitude," returned the gentleman, "a few of us are endeavouring to raise a fund to buy the Poor some meat and drink, and means of warmth. We choose this time, because it is a time, of all others, when Want is keenly felt, and Abundance rejoices. What shall I put you down for?"

"Nothing!" Scrooge replied.

"You wish to be anonymous?"

"I wish to be left alone," said Scrooge. "Since you ask me what I wish, gentlemen, that is my answer. I don't make merry myself at Christmas and I can't afford to make idle people merry. I help to support the establishments I have mentioned—they cost enough; and those who are badly off must go there."

"Many can't go there; and many would rather die."

"If they would rather die," said Scrooge, "they had better do it, and decrease the surplus population. Besides—excuse me—I don't know that."

"But you might know it," observed the gentleman.

"It's not my business," Scrooge returned. "It's enough for a man to understand his own business, and not to interfere with other people's. Mine occupies me constantly. Good afternoon, gentlemen!"

Seeing clearly that it would be useless to pursue their point, the gentlemen withdrew. Scrooge resumed his labours with an improved opinion of himself, and in a more facetious temper than was usual with him.

Meanwhile the fog and darkness thickened so, that people ran about with flaring links, proffering their services to go before horses in carriages, and conduct them on their way. The ancient tower of a church, whose gruff old bell was always peeping slily down at Scrooge out of a gothic window in the wall, became invisible, and struck the hours and quarters in the clouds, with tremulous vibrations afterwards as if its teeth were chattering in its frozen head up there. The cold became intense. In the main street, at the corner of the court, some labourers were repairing the gas-pipes, and had lighted a great fire in a brazier, round which a party of ragged men and boys were gathered: warming their hands and winking their eyes before the blaze in rapture. The water-plug being left in solitude, its overflowings sullenly congealed, and turned to misanthropic ice. The brightness of the shops where holly sprigs and berries crackled in the lamp heat of the windows, made pale faces ruddy as they passed. Poulterers' and grocers' trades became a splendid joke: a glorious pageant, with which it was next to impossible to believe that such dull principles as bargain and sale had anything to do. The Lord Mayor, in the stronghold of the mighty Mansion House, gave orders to his fifty cooks and butlers to keep Christmas as a Lord Mayor's household should; and even the little tailor, whom he had fined five shillings on the previous Monday for being drunk and blood-thirsty in the streets, stirred up to-morrow's pudding in his garret, while his lean wife and the baby sallied out to buy the beef.

Foggier yet, and colder. Piercing, searching, biting cold. If the good Saint Dunstan had but nipped the Evil Spirit's nose with a touch of such weather as that, instead of using his familiar weapons, then indeed he would have roared to lusty purpose. The owner of one scant young nose, gnawed and mumbled by the hungry cold as bones are gnawed by dogs, stooped down at Scrooge's keyhole to regale him with a Christmas carol: but at the first sound of

"God bless you, merry gentleman!
May nothing you dismay!"

Scrooge seized the ruler with such energy of action, that the singer fled in terror, leaving the keyhole to the fog and even more congenial frost.

At length the hour of shutting up the counting-house arrived. With an ill-will Scrooge dismounted from his stool, and tacitly admitted the fact to the expectant clerk in the

Tank, who instantly snuffed his candle out, and put on his hat.

"You'll want all day to-morrow, I suppose?" said Scrooge.

"If quite convenient, sir."

"It's not convenient," said Scrooge, "and it's not fair. If I was to stop half-a-crown for it, you'd think yourself ill-used, I'll be bound?"

The clerk smiled faintly.

"And yet," said Scrooge, "you don't think *me* ill-used, when I pay a day's wages for no work."

The clerk observed that it was only once a year.

"A poor excuse for picking a man's pocket every twenty-fifth of December!" said Scrooge, buttoning his great-coat to the chin. "But I suppose you must have the whole day. Be here all the earlier next morning."

The clerk promised that he would; and Scrooge walked out with a growl. The office was closed in a twinkling, and the clerk, with the long ends of his white comforter dangling below his waist (for he boasted no great-coat), went down a slide on Cornhill, at the end of a lane of boys, twenty times, in honour of its being Christmas Eve, and then ran home to Camden Town as hard as he could pelt, to play at blind-man's-bluff.

Scrooge took his melancholy dinner in his usual melancholy tavern; and having read all the newspapers, and beguiled the rest of the evening with his banker's-book, went home to bed. He lived in chambers which had once belonged to his deceased partner. They were a gloomy suite of rooms, in a lowering pile of building up a yard, where it had so little business to be, that one could scarcely help fancying it must have run there when it was a young house, playing at hide-and-seek with other houses, and forgotten the way out again. It was old enough now, and dreary enough, for nobody lived in it but Scrooge, the other rooms being all let out as offices. The yard was so dark that even Scrooge, who knew its every stone, was fain to grope with his hands. The fog and frost so hung about the black old gateway of the house, that it seemed as if the Genius of the Weather sat in mournful meditation on the threshold.

Now, it is a fact, that there was nothing at all particular about the knocker on the door, except that it was very large. It is also a fact, that Scrooge had seen it, night and morning, during his whole residence in that place; also that Scrooge had as little of what is called fancy about him as any man in the city of London, even including—which is a bold word—the corporation, aldermen, and livery. Let it also be borne in mind that Scrooge had not bestowed one thought on Marley, since his last mention of his seven-years' dead partner that afternoon. And then let any man explain to me, if he can, how it happened that Scrooge, having his key in the lock of the door, saw in the knocker, without its undergoing any intermediate process of change—not a knocker, but Marley's face.

Marley's face. It was not in impenetrable shadow as the other objects in the yard were, but had a dismal light about it, like a bad lobster in a dark cellar. It was not angry or ferocious, but looked at Scrooge as Marley used to look: with ghostly spectacles turned up on its ghostly forehead. The hair was curiously stirred, as if by breath or hot air; and, though the eyes were wide open, they were perfectly motionless. That, and its livid colour, made it horrible; but its horror seemed to be in spite of the face and beyond its control, rather than a part of its own expression.

As Scrooge looked fixedly at this phenomenon, it was a knocker again.

To say that he was not startled, or that his blood was not conscious of a terrible sensation to which it had been a stranger from infancy, would be untrue. But he put his hand upon the key he had relinquished, turned it sturdily, walked in, and lighted his candle.

He *did* pause, with a moment's irresolution, before he shut the door; and he *did* look cautiously behind it first, as if he half expected to be terrified with the sight of Marley's pigtail sticking out into the hall. But there was nothing on the back of the door, except the screws and nuts that held the knocker on, so he said, "Pooh, pooh!" and closed it with a bang.

The sound resounded through the house like thunder. Every room above, and every cask in the wine-merchant's cellars below, appeared to have a separate peal of echoes of its own. Scrooge was not a man to be frightened by echoes. He fastened the door, and walked across the hall, and up the stairs; slowly too: trimming his candle as he went.

You may talk vaguely about driving a coach-and-six up a good old flight of stairs, or through a bad young Act of Parliament; but I mean to say you might have got a hearse up that staircase, and taken it broadwise, with the splinter-bar towards the wall and the door towards the balustrades: and done it easy. There was plenty of width for that, and room to spare; which is perhaps the reason why Scrooge thought he saw a locomotive hearse going on before him in the gloom. Half-a-dozen gas-lamps out of the street wouldn't have lighted the entry too well, so you may suppose that it was pretty dark with Scrooge's dip.

Up Scrooge went, not caring a button for that. Darkness is cheap, and Scrooge liked it. But before he shut his heavy door, he walked through his rooms to see that all was right. He had just enough recollection of the face to desire to do that.

Sitting-room, bed-room, lumber-room. All as they should be. Nobody under the table, nobody under the sofa; a small fire in the grate; spoon and basin ready; and the little saucepan of gruel (Scrooge had a cold in his head) upon the hob. Nobody under the bed; nobody in the closet; nobody in his dressing-gown, which was hanging up in a suspicious attitude against the wall. Lumber-room as usual. Old fire-guard, old shoes, two fish-baskets, washing-stand on three legs, and a poker.

Quite satisfied, he closed his door, and locked himself in; double-locked himself in, which was not his custom. Thus secured against surprise, he took off his cravat; put on his dressing-gown and slippers, and his nightcap; and sat down before the fire to take his gruel.

It was a very low fire indeed; nothing on such a bitter night. He was obliged to sit close to it, and brood over it, before he could extract the least sensation of warmth from such a handful of fuel. The fireplace was an old one, built by some Dutch merchant long ago, and paved all round with quaint Dutch tiles, designed to illustrate the Scriptures. There were Cains and Abels, Pharaoh's daughters, Queens of Sheba, Angelic messengers descending through the air on clouds like feather-beds, Abrahams, Belshazzars, Apostles putting off to sea in butter-boats, hundreds of figures to attract his thoughts; and yet that face of Marley, seven years dead, came like the ancient Prophet's rod, and swallowed up the whole. If each smooth tile had been a blank at first, with power to shape some picture on its surface from the disjointed fragments of his thoughts, there would have been a copy of old Marley's head on every one.

"Humbug!" said Scrooge; and walked across the room.

After several turns, he sat down again. As he threw his head back in the chair, his glance happened to rest upon a bell, a disused bell, that hung in the room, and communicated for some purpose now forgotten with a chamber in the highest story of the building. It was with great astonishment, and with a strange, inexplicable dread, that as he looked, he saw this bell begin to swing. It swung so softly in the outset that it scarcely made a sound; but soon it rang out loudly, and so did every bell in the house.

This might have lasted half a minute, or a minute, but it seemed an hour. The bells ceased as they had begun, together. They were succeeded by a clanking noise, deep down below; as if some person were dragging a heavy chain over the casks in the wine-merchant's cellar. Scrooge then remembered to have heard that ghosts in haunted houses were described as dragging chains.

The cellar-door flew open with a booming sound, and then he heard the noise much louder, on the floors below; then coming up the stairs; then coming straight towards his door.

"It's humbug still!" said Scrooge. "I won't believe it."

His colour changed though, when, without a pause, it came on through the heavy door, and passed into the room before his eyes. Upon its coming in, the dying flame leaped up, as though it cried, "I know him; Marley's Ghost!" and fell again.

The same face: the very same. Marley in his pigtail, usual waistcoat, tights and boots; the tassels on the latter bristling, like his pigtail, and his coat-skirts, and the hair upon his head. The chain he drew was clasped about his middle. It was long, and wound about him like a tail; and it was made (for Scrooge observed it closely) of cash-boxes, keys, padlocks, ledgers, deeds, and heavy purses wrought in steel. His body was transparent; so that Scrooge, observing him, and looking through his waistcoat, could see the two buttons on his coat behind.

Scrooge had often heard it said that Marley had no bowels, but he had never believed it until now.

No, nor did he believe it even now. Though he looked the phantom through and through, and saw it standing before him; though he felt the chilling influence of its death-cold eyes; and marked the very texture of the folded kerchief bound about its head and chin, which wrapper he had not observed before; he was still incredulous, and fought against his senses.

"How now!" said Scrooge, caustic and cold as ever. "What do you want with me?"

"Much!"—Marley's voice, no doubt about it.

"Who are you?"

"Ask me who I *was*."

"Who *were* you then?" said Scrooge, raising his voice. "You're particular, for a shade." He was going to say "*to* a shade," but substituted this, as more appropriate.

"In life I was your partner, Jacob Marley."

"Can you—can you sit down?" asked Scrooge, looking doubtfully at him.

"I can."

"Do it, then."

Scrooge asked the question, because he didn't know whether a ghost so transparent might find himself in a condition to take a chair; and felt that in the event of its being impossible, it might involve the necessity of an embarrassing explanation. But the ghost sat down on the opposite side of the fireplace, as if he were quite used to it.

"You don't believe in me," observed the Ghost.

"I don't," said Scrooge.

"What evidence would you have of my reality beyond that of your senses?"

"I don't know," said Scrooge.

"Why do you doubt your senses?"

"Because," said Scrooge, "a little thing affects them. A slight disorder of the stomach makes them cheats. You may be an undigested bit of beef, a blot of mustard, a crumb of cheese, a fragment of an underdone potato. There's more of gravy than of grave about you, whatever you are!"

Scrooge was not much in the habit of cracking jokes, nor did he feel, in his heart, by any means waggish then. The truth is, that he tried to be smart, as a means of distracting his own attention, and keeping down his terror; for the spectre's voice disturbed the very marrow in his bones.

To sit, staring at those fixed glazed eyes, in silence for a moment, would play, Scrooge felt, the very deuce with him. There was something very awful, too, in the spectre's being provided with an infernal atmosphere of its own. Scrooge could not feel it himself, but this was clearly the case; for though the Ghost sat perfectly motionless, its hair, and skirts, and tassels, were still agitated as by the hot vapour from an oven.

"You see this toothpick?" said Scrooge, returning quickly to the charge, for the reason just assigned; and wishing, though it were only for a second, to divert the vision's stony gaze from himself.

"I do," replied the Ghost.

"You are not looking at it," said Scrooge.

"But I see it," said the Ghost, "notwithstanding."

"Well!" returned Scrooge, "I have but to swallow this, and be for the rest of my days persecuted by a legion of goblins, all of my own creation. Humbug, I tell you! humbug!"

At this the spirit raised a frightful cry, and shook its chain with such a dismal and appalling noise, that Scrooge held on tight to his chair, to save himself from falling in a swoon. But how much greater was his horror, when the phantom taking off the bandage round its head, as if it were too warm to wear in-doors, its lower jaw dropped down upon its breast!

Scrooge fell upon his knees, and clasped his hands before his face.

"Mercy!" he said. "Dreadful apparition, why do you trouble me?"

"Man of the worldly mind!" replied the Ghost, "do you believe in me or not?"

"I do," said Scrooge. "I must. But why do spirits walk the earth, and why do they come to me?"

"It is required of every man," the Ghost returned, "that the spirit within him should walk abroad among his fellowmen, and travel far and wide; and if that spirit goes not forth in life, it is condemned to do so after death. It is doomed to wander through the world—oh, woe is me!—and witness what it cannot share, but might have shared on earth, and turned to happiness!"

Again the spectre raised a cry, and shook its chain and wrung its shadowy hands.

"You are fettered," said Scrooge, trembling. "Tell me why?"

"I wear the chain I forged in life," replied the Ghost. "I made it link by link, and yard by yard; I girded it on of my own free will, and of my own free will I wore it. Is its pattern strange to *you*?"

Scrooge trembled more and more.

"Or would you know," pursued the Ghost, "the weight and length of the strong coil you bear yourself? It was full as heavy and as long as this, seven Christmas Eves ago. You have laboured on it, since. It is a ponderous chain!"

Scrooge glanced about him on the floor, in the expectation of finding himself surrounded by some fifty or sixty fathoms of iron cable: but he could see nothing.

"Jacob," he said, imploringly. "Old Jacob Marley, tell me more. Speak comfort to me, Jacob!"

"I have none to give," the Ghost replied. "It comes from other regions, Ebenezer Scrooge, and is conveyed by other ministers, to other kinds of men. Nor can I tell you what I would. A very little more is all permitted to me. I cannot rest, I cannot stay, I cannot linger anywhere. My spirit never walked beyond our counting-house—mark me!—in life my spirit never roved beyond the narrow limits of our money-changing hole; and weary journeys lie before me!"

It was a habit with Scrooge, whenever he became thoughtful, to put his hands in his breeches pockets. Pondering on what the Ghost had said, he did so now, but without lifting up his eyes, or getting off his knees.

"You must have been very slow about it, Jacob," Scrooge observed, in a business-like manner, though with humility and deference.

"Slow!" the Ghost repeated.

"Seven years dead," mused Scrooge. "And travelling all the time!"

"The whole time," said the Ghost. "No rest, no peace. Incessant torture of remorse."

"You travel fast?" said Scrooge.

"On the wings of the wind," replied the Ghost.

"You might have got over a great quantity of ground in seven years," said Scrooge.

The Ghost, on hearing this, set up another cry, and clanked its chain so hideously in the dead silence of the night, that the Ward would have been justified in indicting it for a nuisance.

"Oh! captive, bound, and double-ironed," cried the phantom, "not to know, that ages of incessant labour by immortal creatures, for this earth must pass into eternity before the good of which it is susceptible is all developed. Not to know that any Christian spirit working kindly in its little sphere, whatever it may be, will find its mortal life too short for its vast means of usefulness. Not to know that no space of regret can make amends for one life's opportunity misused! Yet such was I! Oh! such was I!"

"But you were always a good man of business, Jacob," faltered Scrooge, who now began to apply this to himself.

"Business!" cried the Ghost, wringing its hands again. "Mankind was my business. The common welfare was my business; charity, mercy, forbearance, and benevolence, were, all, my business. The dealings of my trade were but a drop of water in the comprehensive ocean of my business!"

It held up its chain at arm's length, as if that were the cause of all its unavailing grief, and flung it heavily upon the ground again.

"At this time of the rolling year," the spectre said, "I suffer most. Why did I walk through crowds of fellow-beings with my eyes turned down, and never raise them to that blessed Star which led the Wise Men to a poor abode! Were there no poor homes to which its light would have conducted *me*!"

Scrooge was very much dismayed to hear the spectre going on at this rate, and began to quake exceedingly.

"Hear me!" cried the Ghost. "My time is nearly gone."

"I will," said Scrooge. "But don't be hard upon me! Don't be flowery, Jacob! Pray!"

"How it is that I appear before you in a shape that you can see, I may not tell. I have sat invisible beside you many and many a day."

It was not an agreeable idea. Scrooge shivered, and wiped the perspiration from his brow.

"That is no light part of my penance," pursued the Ghost. "I am here to-night to warn you, that you have yet a chance and hope of escaping my fate. A chance and hope of my procuring, Ebenezer."

"You were always a good friend to me," said Scrooge. "Thank'ee!"

"You will be haunted," resumed the Ghost, "by Three Spirits."

Scrooge's countenance fell almost as low as the Ghost's had done.

"Is that the chance and hope you mentioned, Jacob?" he demanded, in a faltering voice.

"It is."

"I—I think I'd rather not," said Scrooge.

"Without their visits," said the Ghost, "you cannot hope to shun the path I tread. Expect the first to-morrow, when the bell tolls One."

"Couldn't I take 'em all at once, and have it over, Jacob?" hinted Scrooge.

"Expect the second on the next night at the same hour. The third upon the next night when the last stroke of Twelve has ceased to vibrate. Look to see me no more; and look that, for your own sake, you remember what has passed between us!"

When it had said these words, the spectre took its wrapper from the table, and bound it round its head, as before. Scrooge knew this, by the smart sound its teeth made, when the jaws were brought together by the bandage. He ventured to raise his eyes again, and found his supernatural visitor confronting him in an erect attitude, with its chain wound over and about its arm.

The apparition walked backward from him; and at every step it took, the window raised itself a little, so that when the spectre reached it, it was wide open.

It beckoned Scrooge to approach, when he did. When they were within two paces of each other, Marley's Ghost held up its hand, warning him to come no nearer. Scrooge stopped.

Not so much in obedience, as in surprise and fear: for on the raising of the hand, he became sensible of confused noises in the air; incoherent sounds of lamentation and regret; wailings inexpressibly sorrowful and self-accusatory. The spectre, after listening for a moment, joined in the mournful dirge; and floated out upon the bleak, dark night.

Scrooge followed to the window: desperate in his curiosity. He looked out.

The air was filled with phantoms, wandering hither and thither in restless haste, and moaning as they went.

Every one of them wore chains like Marley's Ghost; some few (they might be guilty governments) were linked together; none were free. Many had been personally known to Scrooge in their lives. He had been quite familiar with one old ghost, in a white waistcoat, with a monstrous iron safe attached to its ankle, who cried piteously at being unable to assist a wretched woman with an infant, whom it saw below, upon a doorstep. The misery with them all was, clearly, that they sought to interfere, for good, in human matters, and had lost the power for ever.

Whether these creatures faded into mist, or mist enshrouded them, he could not tell. But they and their spirit voices faded together; and the night became as it had been when he walked home.

Scrooge closed the window, and examined the door by which the Ghost had entered. It was double-locked, as he had locked it with his own hands, and the bolts were undisturbed. He tried to say, "Humbug!" but stopped at the first syllable. And being, from the emotion he had undergone, or the fatigues of the day, or his glimpse of the Invisible World, or the dull conversation of the Ghost, or the lateness of the hour, much in need of repose; went straight to bed, without undressing, and fell asleep upon the instant.

God Rest You Merry, Gentlemen

God rest you merry, gentlemen,
Let nothing you dismay,
Remember Christ our Saviour
Was born on Christmas Day,
To save us all from Satan's pow'r,
When we were gone astray.

Chorus
O tidings of comfort and joy,
Comfort and joy,
O tidings of comfort and joy.

From God our heav'nly Father,
A blessed Angel came,
And unto certain shepherds
Brought tidings of the same;
How that in Bethlehem was born
The Son of God by Name.
Chorus

The Shepherds at those tidings
Rejoiced much in mind
And left their flocks a-feeding
In tempest, storm, and wind,
And went straightway to Bethlehem
The Son of God to find.
Chorus

And when they came to Bethlehem,
Where our dear Saviour lay,
They found Him in a manger
Where oxen feed on hay;
His mother Mary kneeling down
Unto the Lord did pray.
Chorus

Now to the Lord sing praises,
All you within this place,
And with true love and brotherhood
Each other now embrace;
This holy tide of Christmas
All other doth deface.
Chorus

OLD ENGLISH CAROL

Mrs. Parkins' Christmas Eve

SARAH ORNE JEWETT

I

One wintry-looking afternoon the sun was getting low, but still shone with cheerful radiance into Mrs. Lydia Parkins' sitting-room. To point out a likeness between the bareness of the room and the appearance of the outside world on that twenty-first of December might seem ungracious; but there was a certain leaflessness and inhospitality common to both.

The cold, gray wall-paper, and dull, thin furniture: the indescribable poverty and lack of comfort of the room were exactly like the leaflessness and sharpness and coldness of that early winter day—unless the sun shone out with a golden glow as it had done in the latter part of the afternoon; then both the room, and the long hillside and frozen road and distant western hills were quite transfigured.

Mrs. Parkins sat upright in one of the six decorous wooden chairs with cane seats; she was trimming a dismal gray-and-black winter bonnet and her work-basket was on the end of the table in front of her, between the windows, with a row of spools on the windowsill at her left. The only luxury she permitted herself was a cricket, a little bench such as one sees in a church pew, with a bit of carpet to cover its top. Mrs. Parkins was so short that she would have been quite off-soundings otherwise in her cane-seated chair; but she had a great horror of persons who put their feet on chair rungs and wore the paint off. She was always on the watch to break the young of this bad habit. She cast a suspicious glance now and then at little Lucy Deems, who sat in another cane-seated chair opposite. The child had called upon Mrs. Parkins before, and was now trying so hard to be good that both her feet had gone to sleep and had come to the prickling stage of that misery. She wondered if her mother were not almost ready to go home.

Mrs. Deems sat in the rocking-chair, full in the sunlight and faced the sun itself, unflinchingly. She was a broad-faced gay-hearted, little woman, and her face was almost as bright as the winter sun itself. One might fancy that they were having a match at trying to outshine one another, but so far it was not Mrs. Deems who blinked and withdrew from the contest. She was just now conscious of little Lucy's depression and anxious looks, and bade her go out to run about a little while and see if there were some of Mrs. Parkins' butternuts left under the big tree.

The door closed, and Mrs. Parkins snapped her thread and said that there was no butternuts out there; perhaps Lucy should have a few in a basket when she was going home.

"Oh, 'taint no matter," said Mrs. Deems, easily. "She was kind of distressed sittin' so quiet; they like to rove about, children does."

"She won't do no mischief?" asked the hostess, timidly.

"Lucy?" laughed the mother. "Why you ought to be better acquainted with Lucy than that, I'm sure. I catch myself wishing she wa'n't quite so still; she takes after her father's folks, all quiet and dutiful, and ain't got the least idea how to enjoy themselves; we was all kind of noisy to our house when I was grown up, and I can't seem to sense the Deems."

"I often wish I had just such a little girl as your Lucy," said Mrs. Parkins, with a sigh. She held her gray-and-black bonnet off with her left hand and looked at it without approval.

"I shall always continue to wear black for Mr. Deems," she said, "but I had this piece of dark-gray ribbon and I thought I had better use it on my black felt; the felt is sort of rusty, now, and black silk trimmings increase the rusty appearance."

"They do so," frankly acknowledged Mrs. Deems. "Why don't you go an' get you a new one for meetin,' Mrs. Parkins? Felts ain't high this season, an' you've got this for second wear."

"I've got one that's plenty good for best," replied Mrs. Parkins, without any change of expression. "It seems best to make this do one more winter." She began to re-arrange the gray ribbon, and Mrs. Deems watched her with a twinkle in her eyes; she had something to say, and did not know exactly how to begin, and Mrs. Parkins knew it as well as she did, and was holding her back which made the occasion more and more difficult.

"There!" she exclaimed at last, boldly, "I expect you know what I've come to see you for, an' I can't set here and make talk no longer. May's well ask if you can do anything about the minister's present."

Mrs. Parkins' mouth was full of pins, and she removed them all, slowly, before she spoke. The sun went behind a low snow cloud along the horizon, and Mrs. Deems shone on alone. It was not very warm in the room, and she gathered her woolen shawl closer about her shoulders as if she were getting ready to go home.

"I don't know's I feel to give you anything to-day, Mrs. Deems," said Mrs. Parkins in a resolved tone. "I don't feel much acquainted with the minister's folks. I must say *she* takes a good deal upon herself; I don't like so much of a ma'am."

"She's one of the pleasantest, best women we ever had in town, *I* think," replied Mrs. Deems. "I was tellin' 'em the other day that I always felt as if she brought a pleasant feelin' wherever she came, so sisterly and own-folks-like. They've seen a sight o' trouble and must feel pinched at times, but she finds ways to do plenty o' kindnesses. I never see a mite of behavior in 'em as if we couldn't do enough for 'em because they was ministers. Some minister's folks has such expectin' ways, and the more you do the more you may; but it ain't so with the Lanes. They are always a thinkin' what they can do for other people, an' they do it, too. You never liked 'em, but I can't see why."

"He ain't the ablest preacher that ever was," said Mrs. Parkins.

"I don't care if he ain't; words is words, but a man that lives as Mr. Lane does, is the best o' ministers," answered Mrs. Deems.

"Well, I don't owe 'em nothin' to-day," said the hostess, looking up. "I haven't got it in mind to do for the minister's folks any more than I have; but I may send 'em some apples or somethin', by'n-bye."

"Jest as you feel," said Mrs. Deems, rising quickly and looking provoked. "I didn't know but what 'twould be a pleasure to you, same's 'tis to the rest of us."

"They ain't been here very long, and I pay my part to the salary, an' 'taint no use to overdo in such cases."

"They've been put to extra expense this fall, and have been very feeling and kind; real interested in all of us, and such a help to the parish as we ain't had for a good while before. Havin' to send their boy to the hospital, has made it hard for 'em."

"Well, folks has to have their hard times, and minister's families can't escape. I am sorry about the boy, I'm sure," said Mrs. Parkins, generously. "Don't you go, Mrs. Deems; you ain't been to see me for a good while. I want you to see my bonnet in jest a minute."

"I've got to go way over to the Dilby's, and it's goin' to be dark early. I should be pleased to have you come an' see me. I've got to find Lucy and trudge along."

"I believe I won't rise to see you out o' the door, my lap's so full," said Mrs. Parkins politely, and so they parted. Lucy was hopping up and down by the front fence to keep herself warm and occupied.

"She didn't say anything about the butternuts, did she, mother?" the child asked; and Mrs. Deems laughed and shook her head. Then they walked away down the road together, the big-mittened hand holding fast the little one, and the hooded heads bobbing toward each other now and then, as if they were holding a lively conversation. Mrs. Parkins looked after them two or three times, suspiciously at first, as if she thought they might be talking about her; then a little wistfully. She had come of a saving family and had married a saving man.

"Isn't Mrs. Parkins real poor, mother?" little Lucy inquired in a compassionate voice.

Mrs. Deems smiled, and assured the child that there was nobody so well off in town except Colonel Drummond, so far as money went; but Mrs. Parkins took care neither to enjoy her means herself, nor to let anybody else. Lucy pondered this strange answer for a while and then began to hop and skip along the rough road, still holding fast her mother's warm hand.

This was the twenty-first of December, and the day of the week was Monday. On Tuesday Mrs. Parkins did her frugal ironing, and on Wednesday she meant to go over to Haybury to put some money into the bank and to do a little shopping. Goods were cheaper in Haybury in some of the large stores, than they were at the corner store at home, and she had the horse and could always get dinner at her cousin's. To be sure, the cousin was always hinting for presents for herself or her children, but Mrs. Parkins could bear that, and always cleared her conscience by asking the boys over in haying-time, though their help cost more than it came to with their growing appetites and the wear and tear of the house. Their mother came for a day's visit now and then, but everything at home depended upon her hard-working hands, as she had been early left a widow with little else to depend upon, until now, when the boys were out of school. One was doing well in the shoe factory and one in a store. Mrs. Parkins was really much attached to her cousin, but she thought if she once began to give, they would always be expecting something.

As has been said, Wednesday was the day set for the visit, but when Wednesday came it was a hard winter day, cold and windy, with an occasional flurry of snow, and Mrs. Parkins being neuralgic, gave up going until Thursday. She was pleased when she waked Thursday morning to find the weather warmer and the wind stilled. She was weather-wise enough to see snow in the clouds, but it was only eight miles to Haybury and she could start early and come home again as soon as she got her dinner. So the boy who came every morning to take care of her horse and bring in wood, was hurried and urged until he nearly lost his breath, and the horse was put into the wagon and, with rare forethought, a piece of salt-pork was wrapped up and put under the wagon-seat; then with a cloud over the re-trimmed bonnet, and a shawl over her Sunday cloak, and mittens over her woolen gloves Mrs. Parkins drove away. All her neighbors knew that she was going to Haybury to put eighty-seven dollars into the bank that the Dilby brothers had paid her for some rye planted and harvested on the halves. Very likely she had a good deal of money beside, that day; she had the best farm in that sterile neighborhood and was a famous manager.

The cousin was a hospitable, kindly soul, very loyal to her relations and always ready with a welcome. Beside, though the ears of Lydia Parkins were deaf to hints of present need and desire, it was more than likely that she would leave her farm and savings to the boys; she was not a person to speak roughly to, or one whom it was possible to disdain. More than this, no truly compassionate heart could fail to pity the thin, anxious, forbidding little woman, who behaved as if she must always be on the defensive against a plundering and begging world.

Cousin Mary Faber, as usual, begged Mrs. Parkins to spend the night; she seemed to take so little pleasure in life that the change might do her good. There would be no expense except for the horse's stabling, Mrs. Faber urged openly, and nobody would be expecting her at home. But Mrs. Parkins, as usual refused, and feared that the cellar would freeze. It had not been banked up as she liked to have it that autumn, but as for paying the Dilby's a dollar and a quarter for doing it, she didn't mean to please them so much.

"Land sakes! Why don't you feel as rich as you be, an' not mind them little expenses?" said cousin Faber, daringly. "I do declare I don't see how you can make out to grow richer an' poorer at the same time." The good-natured soul could not help laughing as she spoke, and Mrs. Parkins herself really could not help smiling.

"I'm much obliged to you for the pleasure of your company," said cousin Faber, "and it was very considerate of you to bring me that nice piece o' pork." If she had only known what an effort her guest had made to carry it into the house after she had brought it! Twice Mrs. Parkins had pushed it back under the wagon seat with lingering indecision, and only taken it out at last because she feared that one of those prowling boys might discover it in the wagon and tell his mother. How often she had taken something into her hand to give away and then put it back and taken it again half a dozen times, irresolutely. There were still blind movements of the heart toward generosity, but she had grown more and more skillful at soothing her conscience and finding excuses for not giving.

The Christmas preparations in the busy little town made her uncomfortable, and cheerful cousin Faber's happiness in her own pinched housekeeping was a rebuke. The boys' salaries were very small indeed, this first year or two; but their mother was proud of their steadiness, and still sewed and let rooms to lodgers and did everything she could to earn money. She looked tired and old before her time, and acknowledged to Mrs. Parkins that she should like to have a good, long visit at the farm the next summer and let the boys take their meals with a neighbor. "I never spared myself one step until they were through with their schooling; but now it will be so I can take things a little easier," said the good soul with a wistful tone that was unusual.

Mrs. Parkins felt impatient as she listened; she knew that a small present of money now and then would have been a great help, but she never could make up her mind to begin what promised to be the squandering of her carefully saved fortune. It would be the ruin of the boys, too, if they thought she could be appealed to in every emergency. She would make it up to them in the long run; she could not take her money with her to the next world, and she would make a virtue of necessity.

The afternoon was closing in cold and dark, and the snow came sifting down slowly before Mrs. Parkins was out of the street of Haybury. She had lived too long on a hill not to be weather-wise, and for a moment, as the wind buffeted her face and she saw the sky and the horizon line all dulled by the coming storm, she had a great mind to go back to cousin Faber's. If it had been any other time in the year but Christmas eve! The old horse gathered his forces and hurried along as if he had sense enough to be anxious about the weather; but presently the road turned so that the wind was not so chilling and they were quickly out of sight of the town, crossing the level land which lay between Haybury and the hills of Holton. Mrs. Parkins was persuaded that she should get home by dark, and the old horse did his very best. The road was rough and frozen and the wagon rattled as it pitched along; it was like a race between Mrs. Parkins and the storm, and for a time it seemed certain that she would be the winner.

The gathering forces of the wind did not assert themselves fully until nearly half the eight miles had been passed, and the snow which had only clung to Mrs. Parkins' blanket-shawl like a white veil at first, and sifted white across the frozen grass of the lowlands, lay at last like a drift on the worn buffalo-robe, and was so deep in the road that it began to clog the wheels. It was a most surprising snow in the thickness of the flakes and the rapidity with which it gathered; it was no use to try to keep the white-knitted cloud over her face, for it became so thick with snow that it blinded and half-stifled her. The darkness began to fall, the snow came thicker and faster, and the horse climbing the drifted hills with the snow-clogged old wagon, had to stop again and again. The awful thought suddenly came to Mrs. Parkins' mind that she could not reach home that night, and the next moment she had to acknowledge that she did not know exactly where she was. The thick flakes blinded her; she turned to look behind to see if anyone were coming; but she might have been in the middle of an Arctic waste. She felt benumbed and stupid, and again tried to urge the tired horse, and the good creature toiled on desperately. It seemed as if they must have left the lowland far enough behind to be near some houses, but it grew still darker and snowier as they dragged slowly for another mile until it was impossible to get any further, and the horse stopped still and then gave a shake to rid himself of the drift on his back, and turned his head to look inquiringly at his mistress.

Mrs. Parkins began to cry with cold, and fear and misery. She had read accounts of such terrible, sudden storms in the west, and here she was in the night, foodless, and shelterless, and helpless.

"Oh! I'd give a thousand dollars to be safe under cover!" groaned the poor soul. "Oh, how poor I be this minute, and I come right away from that warm house!"

A strange dazzle of light troubled her eyes, and a vision of the brightly-lighted Haybury shops, and the merry customers that were hurrying in and out, and the gayety and contagious generosity of Christmas eve mocked at the stingy, little lost woman as she sat there half bewildered. The heavy flakes of snow caught her eyelashes and chilled her cheeks and melted inside the gray bonnet-strings; they heaped themselves on the top of the bonnet into a high crown that toppled into her lap as she moved. If she tried to brush the snow away, her clogged mitten only gathered more and grew more and more clumsy. It was a horrible, persistent storm; at this rate the horse and driver both would soon be covered and frozen in the road. The gathering flakes were malicious and mysterious; they were so large and flaked so fast down out of the sky.

"My goodness! How numb I be this minute," whispered

Mrs. Parkins. And then she remembered that the cashier of the bank had told her that morning when she made her deposit, that everybody else was taking out their money that day; she was the only one who had come to put any in.

"I'd pay every cent of it willin' to anybody that would come along and help me get to shelter," said the poor soul. "Oh, I don't know as I've hoed so's to be worth savin' "; and a miserable sense of shame and defeat beat down whatever hope tried to rise in her heart. What had she tried to do for God and man that gave her a right to think of love and succor now?

Yet it seemed every moment as if help must come and as if this great emergency could not be so serious. Life had been so montonous to Mrs. Parkins, so destitute of excitement and tragic situations that she could hardly understand, even now, that she was in such great danger. Again she called as loud as she could for help, and the horse whinnied louder still. The only hope was that two men who had passed her some miles back would remember that they had advised her to hurry, and would come back to look for her. The poor, old horse had dragged himself and the wagon to the side of the road under the shelter of some evergreens; Mrs. Parkins slipped down under the buffalo into the bottom of her cold, old wagon, and covered herself as well as she could. There was more than a chance that she might be found frozen under a snow-drift in the morning.

The morning! Christmas morning!

What did the advent of Christmas day hold out for her—buried in the snow-drifts of a December storm!

Anything? Yes, but she knew it not. Little did she dream what this Christmas eve was to bring into her life!

II

Lydia Parkins was a small woman of no great vigor, but as she grew a little warmer under her bed of blankets in the bottom of the old wagon, she came to her senses. She must get out and try to walk on through the snow as far as she could; it was no use to die there in this fearful storm like a rabbit. Yes, and she must unharness the horse and let him find his way; so she climbed boldly down into the knee-deep snow where a drift had blown already. She would not admit the thought that perhaps she might be lost in the snow and frozen to death that very night. It did not seem in character with Mrs. Nathan Parkins, who was the owner of plenty of money in Haybury Bank, and a good farm well divided into tillage and woodland, who had plenty of blankets and comforters at home, and firewood enough, and suitable winter clothes to protect her from the weather. The wind was rising more and more, it made the wet gray-and-black bonnet feel very limp and cold about her head, and her poor head itself felt duller and heavier than ever. She lost one glove and mitten in the snow as she tried to unharness the old horse, and her bare fingers were very clumsy, but she managed to get the good old creature clear, hoping that he would plod on and be known farther along the road and get help for her; but instead of that he only went round and round her and the wagon, floundering and whinnying, and refusing to be driven away. "What kind of a storm is this going to be?" groaned Mrs. Parkins, wading along the road and falling over her dress helplessly. The old horse meekly followed and when she gave a weak, shrill, womanish shout, old Major neighed and shook the snow off his back. Mrs. Parkins knew in her inmost heart, that with such a wind and through such drifts she could not get very far, and at last she lost her breath and sank down at the roadside and the horse went on alone. It was horribly dark and the cold pierced her through and through. In a few minutes she staggered to her feet and went on; she could have cried because the horse was out of sight, but she found it easier following in his tracks.

Suddenly there was a faint twinkle of light on the left, and what a welcome sight it was! The poor wayfarer hastened, but the wind behaved as if it were trying to blow her back. The horse had reached shelter first and somebody had heard him outside and came out and shut the house door with a loud bang that reached Mrs. Parkins' ears. She tried to shout again but she could hardly make a sound. The light still looked a good way off, but presently she could hear voices and see another light moving. She was so tired that she must wait until they came to help her. Who lived in the first house on the left after you passed oak ridge? Why, it couldn't be the Donnells, for they were all away in Haybury, and the house was shut up; this must be the parsonage, and she was off the straight road home. The bewildered horse had taken the left-hand road. "Well," thought Mrs. Parkins, "I'd rather be most anywhere else, but I don't care where 'tis so long as I get under cover. I'm all spent and wore out."

The lantern came bobbing along quickly as if somebody were hurrying, and wavered from side to side as if it were in a fishing boat on a rough sea. Mrs. Parkins started to meet it, and made herself known to her rescuer.

"I declare, if 'taint the minister," she exclaimed. "I'm Mrs. Parkins, or what's left of her. I've come near bein' froze to death along back here a-piece. I never saw such a storm in all my life."

She sank down in the snow and could not get to her feet again. The minister was a strong man, he stooped and lifted her like a child and carried her along the road with the lantern hung on his arm. She was a little woman and she was not a person given to sentiment, but she had been dreadfully cold and frightened, and now at last she was safe. It was like the good shepherd in the Bible, and Lydia Parkins was past crying; but it seemed as if she could never speak again and as if her heart were going to break. It seemed inevitable that the minister should have come to find her and carry her to the fold; no, to the parsonage; but she felt dizzy and strange again, and the second-best gray-and-black bonnet slipped its knot and tumbled off into the snow without her knowing it.

When Mrs. Parkins opened her eyes a bright light made them shut again directly; then she discovered, a moment afterward, that she was in the parsonage sitting-room and the minister's wife was kneeling beside her with an anxious face; and there was a Christmas tree at the other side of the room, with all its pretty, shining things and gay little candles on the boughs. She was comfortably wrapped in warm blankets, but she felt very tired and weak. The minister's wife smiled with delight: "Now you'll feel all right in a few minutes," she exclaimed. "Think of your being out in this awful storm! Don't try to talk to us yet, dear," she added kindly, "I'm going to bring you a cup of good hot tea. Are you all right? Don't try to tell anything about the storm. Mr. Lane has seen to the horse. Here, I'll put my little red shawl over you, it looks prettier than the blankets, and I'm drying your clothes in the kitchen."

The minister's wife had a sweet face; and she stood for a minute looking down at her unexpected guest; then something in the thin, appealing face on the sofa seemed to touch her heart, and she stooped over and kissed Mrs. Parkins. It happened that nobody had kissed Mrs. Parkins for years, and the tears stole down her cheeks as Mrs. Lane turned away.

As for the minister's wife, she had often thought that Mrs. Parkins had a most disagreeable hard face; she liked her less than any one in the parish, but now as she brightened the kitchen fire, she began to wonder what she could find to put on the Christmas tree for her, and wondered why she never had noticed a frightened, timid look in the poor woman's eyes. "It is so forlorn for her to live all alone on that big farm," said Mrs. Lane to herself, mindful of her own happy home and the children. All three of them came close about their mother at that moment, lame-footed John with his manly pale face, and smiling little Bell and Mary, the girls.

The minister came in from the barn and blew his lantern out and hung it away. The old horse was blanketed as warm as his mistress, and there was a good supper in his crib. It was a very happy household at the parsonage, and Mrs. Parkins could hear their whispers and smothered laughter in the kitchen. It was only eight o'clock after all, and it was evident that the children longed to begin their delayed festivities. The little girls came and stood in the doorway and looked first at the stranger guest and then at their Christmas tree, and after a while their mother came with them to ask whether Mrs. Parkins felt equal to looking on at the pleasuring or whether she would rather go to bed and rest, and sleep away her fatigue.

Mrs. Parkins wished to look on; she was beginning to feel well again, but she dreaded being alone, she could not tell exactly why.

"Come right into the bedroom with me then," said Mrs. Lane, "and put on a nice warm, double gown of mine; 'twill be large enough for you, that's certain, and then if you do wish to move about by-and-by, you will be better able than in the blankets."

Mrs. Parkins felt dazed by this little excitement, yet she was strangely in the mood for it. The reaction of being in this safe and pleasant place, after the recent cold and danger, excited her, and gave her an unwonted power of enjoyment and sympathy. She felt pleased and young, and she wondered what was going to happen. She stood still and let Mrs. Lane brush her gray hair, all tangled with the snow damp, as if she were no older than the little girls themselves; then they went out again to the sitting-room. There was a great fire blazing in the Franklin stove; the minister had cleared a rough bit of the parsonage land the summer before and shown good spirit about it, and these, as Mrs. Parkins saw at once, were some of the pitch-pine roots. She had said when she heard of his hard work, that he had better put the time into his sermons, and she remembered that now with a pang at her heart, and confessed inwardly that she had been mean spirited sometimes toward the Lanes, and it was a good lesson to her to be put at their mercy now. As she sat in her corner by the old sofa in the warm double gown and watched their kindly faces, a new sense of friendliness and hopefulness stole into her heart. "I'm just as warm now as I was cold a while ago," she assured the minister.

The children sat side by side, the lame boy and the two little sisters before the fire, and Mrs. Lane sat on the sofa by Mrs. Parkins, and the minister turned over the leaves of a Bible that lay on the table. It did not seem like a stiff and formal meeting held half from superstition and only half from reverence, but it was as if the good man were telling his household news of some one they all loved and held close to their hearts. He said a few words about the birth of Christ, and of there being no room that night in the inn. Room enough for the Roman soldier and the priest and the tax-gatherer, but no room for Christ; and how we all blame that inn-keeper, and then are like him too often in the busy inn of our hearts. "Room for our friends and our pleasures and our gains, and no room for Christ," said the minister sadly, as the children looked soberly into the fire and tried to understand. Then they heard again the story of the shepherds and the star, and it was a more beautiful story than ever, and seemed quite new and wonderful; and then the minister prayed, and gave special thanks for the friend who made one of their household that night, because she had come through such great danger. Afterward the Lanes sang their Christmas hymn, standing about a little old organ which the mother played: "While shepherds watched their flocks by night—"

They sang it all together as if they loved the hymn, and when they stopped and the room was still again, Mrs. Parkins could hear the wind blow outside and the great elm branches sway and creak above the little house, and the snow clicked busily against the windows. There was a curious warmth at her heart; she did not feel frightened or lonely, or cold, or even selfish any more.

They lighted the candles on the Christmas tree, and the young people capered about and were brimming over with secrets and shouted with delight, and the tree shown and glistened brave in its gay trimming of walnuts covered with gold and silver paper, and little bags sewed with bright worsteds, and all sorts of pretty home-made trifles. But when the real presents were discovered, the presents that meant no end of thought and management and secret self-denial, the brightest part of the household love and happiness shone out. One after another they came to bring Mrs. Parkins her share of the little tree's fruit until her lap was full as she sat on the sofa. One little girl brought a bag of candy, though there wasn't much candy on the tree; and the other gave her a book-mark, and the lame boy had a pretty geranium, grown by himself, with a flower on it, and came limping to put it in her hands; and Mrs. Lane brought a pretty hood that her sister had made for her a few weeks before, but her old one was still good and she did not need two. The minister had found a little book of hymns which a friend had given him at the autumn conference, and as Mrs. Parkins opened it, she happened to see these words: "Room to deny ourselves." She didn't know why the tears rushed to her eyes: "I've got to learn to deny myself of being mean," she thought, almost angrily. It was the least she could do, to do something friendly for these kind people; they had taken her in out of the storm with such loving warmth of sympathy; they did not show the least consciousness that she had never spoken a kind word about them since they came to town; that she alone had held aloof when this dear boy, their only son, had fought through an illness which might leave him a cripple for life. She had heard that there was a hope of his being cured if by-and-by his father could carry him to New York to a famous surgeon there. But all the expense of the long journey and many weeks of treatment, had seemed impossible. They were so thankful to have him still alive and with them that Christmas night. Mrs. Parkins could see the mother's eyes shine with tears as she looked at him, and the father put out a loving hand to steady him as he limped across the room.

"I wish little Lucy Deems, that lives near neighbor to me, was here to help your girls keep Christmas," said Mrs. Parkins, speaking half unconsciously. "Her mother has had it very hard; I mean to bring her over some day when the traveling gets good."

"We know Lucy Deems," said the children with satisfaction. Then Mrs. Parkins thought with regret of cousin Faber and her two boys and was sorry that they were not all at the minister's too. She seemed to have entered upon a new life: she even thought of her dreary home with disapproval, and of its comfortable provisioning in cellar and garret and of her money in the Haybury bank, with secret shame. Here she was with Mrs. Lane's double gown on, as poor a woman as there was in the world; she had come like a beggar to the Lanes' door that Christmas eve, and they were eagerly giving her house-room and gifts great and small: where were her independence and her riches now? She was a stranger and they had taken her in, and they did it for Christ's sake, and he would bless them, but what was there to say for herself? "Lord, how poor I be!" faltered Lydia Parkins for the second time that night.

There had not been such a storm for years. It was days before people could hear from each other along the blockaded country roads. Men were frozen to death, and cattle; and the telegraph wires were down and the safe and comfortable country side felt as if it had been in the power of some merciless and furious force of nature from which it could never again feel secure. But the sun came out and the bluejays came back, and the crows, and the white snow melted, and the farmers went to and fro again along the highways. A new peace and good-will showed itself between the neighbors after their separation, but Mrs. Parkins' good-will outshown the rest. She went to Haybury as soon as the roads were well broken, and brought cousin Faber back with her for a visit, and sent her home again with a loaded wagon of supplies. She called in Lucy Deems and gave her a peck basketful of butternuts on New Year's Day, and told her to come for more when these were gone; and, more than all, one Sunday soon afterwards the minister told his people that he should be away for the next two Sundays. The kindness of a friend was going to put a great blessing within his reach, and he added simply, in a faltering voice, that he hoped all his friends would pray for the restoration to health of his dear boy.

Mrs. Parkins sat in her pew; she had not worn so grim an expression since before Christmas. Nobody could tell what secret pangs these gifts and others like them had cost her, yet she knew that only a right way of living would give her peace of mind. She could no longer live in a mean, narrow world of her own making; she must try to take the world as it is, and make the most of her life.

There were those who laughed and said that her stingy ways were frightened out of her on the night of the storm; but sometimes one is taught and led slowly to a higher level of existence unconsciously and irresistibly, and the decisive upward step once taken is seldom retraced. It was not long before Mrs. Deems said to a neighbor cheerfully: "Why, I always knew Mrs. Parkins meant well enough, but she *didn't know how* to do for other folks; she seemed kind of scared to use her own money as if she didn't have any right to it. Now she is kind of persuaded that she's got the whole responsibility, and just you see how pleased she behaves.

She's just a-beginnin' to live; she never heard one word o' the first prayer yesterday mornin'; I see her beamin' an' smilin' at the minister's boy from the minute she see him walk up the aisle straight an' well as anybody."

"She goin' to have one of her cousin Faber's sons come over and stop awhile, I hear. He got run down workin' in the shoe factory to Haybury. Perhaps he may take hold and she'll let him take the farm by-an'-by. There, we mustn't expect too much of her," said the other woman compassionately. "I'm sure 'tis a blessed change as far as she's got a'ready. Habits'll live sometimes after they're dead. Folks don't find it so easy to go free of ways they've settled into; life's truly a warfare, ain't it?"

"It is, so," answered Mrs. Deems, soberly. "There comes Mrs. Parkins this minute, in the old wagon, and my Lucy settin' up 'longside of her as pert as Nathan! Now ain't Mrs. Parkins' countenance got a pleasanter look than it used to wear? Well, the more she does for others, and the poorer she gets, the richer she seems to feel."

"It's a very unusual circumstance for a woman o' her age to turn right about in her tracks. It makes us believe that Heaven takes hold and helps folks," said the neighbor; and they watched the thin, little woman out of sight along the hilly road with a look of pleased wonder on their own faces. It was mid-spring, but Mrs. Parkins still wore her best winter bonnet; as for the old rusty one trimmed with gray, the minister's little girls found it when the snow drifts melted, and carefully hid it away to deck the parsonage scarecrow in the time of corn-planting.

Christmas Day

I wonder on that Christmas night
   How many passers-by
Beheld that strange and lustrous light
   In Bethlehem's patch of sky?
We know how the shepherds chanced to be
   Unto the stable sent,
But did that star some rich man see
   And wonder what it meant?

They've told us of the crowded inn
   And of the laughter gay;
But was there none who entered in
   On that first Christmas Day
To say he'd seen a wondrous sight
   And bear the news to them
That God had hung a beacon light
   High over Bethlehem?

Of all the throng that hurried by
   Did no one lift his eyes
To read the glory of the sky?
   Were all so worldly-wise
That God should bid the angels sing,
   Upon that midnight clear,
An anthem to the new-born King
   And only shepherds hear?

I wonder is it still the same?
Are we beyond His reach?
Have we, pursuing wealth and fame,
Grown deaf to gentler speech?
Should such a strange thing come to be
And angel choirs appear,
Would only watchful shepherds see
And thoughtful shepherds hear?

EDGAR GUEST

The Oxen

Christmas Eve, and twelve of the clock.
'Now they are all on their knees,'
An elder said as we sat in a flock
By the embers in hearthside ease.

We pictured the meek mild creatures where
They dwelt in their strawy pen,
Nor did it occur to one of us there
To doubt they were kneeling then.

So fair a fancy few would weave
In these years! Yet, I feel,
If someone said on Christmas Eve,
'Come; see the oxen kneel

'In the lonely barton by yonder coomb
Our childhood used to know,'
I should go with him in the gloom,
Hoping it might be so.

THOMAS HARDY

The Child Jesus

Welcome that star in Judah's sky,
  That voice o'er Bethlehem's palmy glen:
The lamp far sages hailed on high,
  The tones that thrilled the shepherd men:
Glory to God in loftiest heaven!
  Thus angels smote the echoing chord;
Glad tidings unto man forgiven,
  Peace from the presence of the Lord.

The Shepherds sought that birth divine,
  The Wise Men traced their guided way;
There, by strange light and mystic sign,
  The God they came to worship lay.
A human Babe in beauty smiled,
  Where lowing oxen round him trod:
A maiden clasped her Awful Child,
  Pure offspring of the breath of God.

Those voices from on high are mute,
  The star the Wise Men saw is dim;
But hope still guides the wanderer's foot,
  And faith renews the angel hymn:
Glory to God in loftiest heaven!
  Touch with glad hand the ancient chord;
Good tidings unto man forgiven,
  Peace from the presence of the Lord.

ROBERT STEPHEN HAWKER

The Gift of the Magi

O. HENRY

One dollar and eighty-seven cents. That was all. And sixty cents of it was in pennies. Pennies saved one and two at a time by bulldozing the grocer and the vegetable man and the butcher until one's cheeks burned with the silent imputation of parsimony that such close dealing implied. Three times Della counted it. One dollar and eighty-seven cents. And the next day would be Christmas.

There was clearly nothing to do but flop down on the shabby little couch and howl. So Della did it. Which instigates the moral reflection that life is made up of sobs, sniffles, and smiles, with sniffles predominating.

While the mistress of the home is gradually subsiding from the first stage to the second, take a look at the home. A furnished flat at $8 per week. It did not exactly beggar description, but it certainly had that word on the lookout for the mendicancy squad.

In the vestibule below was a letter-box into which no letter would go, and an electric button from which no mortal finger could coax a ring. Also appertaining thereunto was a card bearing the name "Mr. James Dillingham Young."

The "Dillingham" had been flung to the breeze during a former period of prosperity when its possessor was being paid $30 per week. Now, when the income was shrunk to $20, the letters of "Dillingham" looked blurred, as though they were thinking seriously of contracting to a modest and unassuming D. But whenever Mr. James Dillingham Young came home and reached his flat above he was called "Jim" and greatly hugged by Mrs. James Dillingham Young, already introduced to you as Della. Which is all very good.

Della finished her cry and attended to her cheeks with the powder rag. She stood by the window and looked out dully at a gray cat walking a gray fence in a gray backyard. Tomorrow would be Christmas Day, and she had only $1.87 with which to buy Jim a present. She had been saving every penny she could for months, with this result. Twenty dollars a week doesn't go far. Expenses had been greater than she had calculated. They always are. Only $1.87 to buy a present for Jim. Her Jim. Many a happy hour she had spent planning for something nice for him. Something fine and rare and sterling—something just a little bit near to being worthy of the honor of being owned by Jim.

There was a pier-glass between the windows of the room. Perhaps you have seen a pier-glass in an $8 flat. A very thin and very agile person may, by observing his reflection in a rapid sequence of longitudinal strips, obtain a fairly accurate conception of his looks. Della, being slender, had mastered the art.

Suddenly she whirled from the window and stood before the glass. Her eyes were shining brilliantly, but her face had lost its color within twenty seconds. Rapidly she pulled down her hair and let it fall to its full length.

Now, there were two possessions of the James Dillingham Youngs in which they both took a mighty pride. One was Jim's gold watch that had been his father's and his grandfather's. The other was Della's hair. Had the Queen of Sheba lived in the flat across the airshaft, Della would have let her hair hang out the window some day to dry just to depreciate Her Majesty's jewels and gifts. Had King Solomon been the janitor, with all his treasures piled up in the basement, Jim would have pulled out his watch every time he passed, just to see him pluck at his beard from envy.

So now Della's beautiful hair fell about her, rippling and shining like a cascade of brown waters. It reached below her knee and made itself almost a garment for her. And then she did it up again nervously and quickly. Once she faltered for a minute and stood still while a tear or two splashed on the worn red carpet.

On went her old brown jacket; on went her old brown hat. With a whirl of skirts and with the brilliant sparkle still in her eyes, she fluttered out the door and down the stairs to the street.

Where she stopped the sign read: "Mme. Sofronie. Hair

Goods of All Kinds." One flight up Della ran, and collected herself, panting. Madame, large, too white, chilly, hardly looked the "Sofronie."

"Will you buy my hair?" asked Della.

"I buy hair," said Madame. "Take yer hat off and let's have a sight at the looks of it."

Down rippled the brown cascade.

"Twenty dollars," said Madame, lifting the mass with a practised hand.

"Give it to me quick," said Della.

Oh, and the next two hours tripped by on rosy wings. Forget the hashed metaphor. She was ransacking the stores for Jim's present.

She found it at last. It surely had been made for Jim and no one else. There was no other like it in any of the stores, and she had turned all of them inside out. It was a platinum fob chain simple and chaste in design, properly proclaiming its value by substance alone and not by meretricious ornamentation—as all good things should do. It was even worthy of The Watch. As soon as she saw it she knew that it must be Jim's. It was like him. Quietness and value—the description applied to both. Twenty-one dollars they took from her for it, and she hurried home with the 87 cents. With that chain on his watch Jim might be properly anxious about the time in any company. Grand as the watch was, he sometimes looked at it on the sly on account of the old leather strap that he used in place of a chain.

When Della reached home her intoxication gave way a little to prudence and reason. She got out her curling irons and lighted the gas and went to work repairing the ravages made by generosity added to love. Which is always a tremendous task, dear friends—a mammoth task.

Within forty minutes her head was covered with tiny, close-lying curls that made her look wonderfully like a truant schoolboy. She looked at her reflection in the mirror long, carefully, and critically.

"If Jim doesn't kill me," she said to herself, "before he takes a second look at me, he'll say I look like a Coney Island chorus girl. But what could I do—oh! what could I do with a dollar and eighty-seven cents?"

At 7 o'clock the coffee was made and the frying-pan was on the back of the stove hot and ready to cook the chops.

Jim was never late. Della doubled the fob chain in her hand and sat on the corner of the table near the door that he always entered. Then she heard his step on the stair away down on the first flight, and she turned white for just a moment. She had a habit of saying little silent prayers about the simplest everyday things, and now she whispered: "Please God, make him think I am still pretty."

The door opened and Jim stepped in and closed it. He looked thin and very serious. Poor fellow, he was only twenty-two—and to be burdened with a family! He needed a new overcoat and he was without gloves.

Jim stopped inside the door, as immovable as a setter at the scent of quail. His eyes were fixed upon Della, and there was an expression in them that she could not read, and it terrified her. It was not anger, nor surprise, nor disapproval, nor horror, nor any of the sentiments that she had been prepared for. He simply stared at her fixedly with that peculiar expression on his face.

Della wriggled off the table and went for him.

"Jim, darling," she cried, "don't look at me that way. I had my hair cut off and sold it because I couldn't have lived through Christmas without giving you a present. It'll grow out again—you won't mind, will you? I just had to do it. My hair grows awfully fast. Say 'Merry Christmas!' Jim, and let's be happy. You don't know what a nice—what a beautiful, nice gift I've got for you."

"You've cut off your hair?" asked Jim, laboriously, as if he had not arrived at that patent fact yet even after the hardest mental labor.

"Cut it off and sold it," said Della. "Don't you like me just as well, anyhow? I'm me without my hair, ain't I?"

Jim looked about the room curiously.

"You say your hair is gone?" he said, with an air almost of idiocy.

"You needn't look for it," said Della. "It's sold, I tell you—sold and gone, too. It's Christmas Eve, boy. Be good to me, for it went for you. Maybe the hairs of my head were numbered," she went on with a sudden serious sweetness, "but nobody could ever count my love for you. Shall I put the chops on, Jim?"

Out of his trance Jim seemed quickly to wake. He enfolded his Della. For ten seconds let us regard with discreet scrutiny some inconsequential object in the other direction. Eight dollars a week or a million a year—what is the difference? A mathematician or a wit would give you the wrong answer. The magi brought valuable gifts, but that was not among them. This dark assertion will be illuminated later on.

Jim drew a package from his overcoat pocket and threw it upon the table.

"Don't make any mistake, Dell," he said, "about me. I don't think there's anything in the way of a haircut or a shave or a shampoo that could make me like my girl any less. But if you'll unwrap that package you may see why you had me going a while at first."

White fingers and nimble tore at the string and paper. And then an ecstatic scream of joy; and then, alas! a quick feminine change to hysterical tears and wails, necessitating the immediate employment of all the comforting powers of the lord of the flat.

For there lay The Combs—the set of combs, side and back, that Della had worshipped for long in a Broadway window. Beautiful combs, pure tortoise shell, with jewelled rims—just the shade to wear in the beautiful vanished hair. They were expensive combs, she knew, and her heart had simply craved and yearned over them without the least hope of possession. And now, they were hers, but the tresses that should have adorned the coveted adornments were gone.

But she hugged them to her bosom, and at length she was able to look up with dim eyes and a smile and say: "My hair grows so fast, Jim!"

And then Della leaped up like a little singed cat and cried, "Oh, oh!"

Jim had not yet seen his beautiful present. She held it out to him eagerly upon her open palm. The dull precious metal seemed to flash with a reflection of her bright and ardent spirit.

"Isn't it a dandy, Jim? I hunted all over town to find it. You'll have to look at the time a hundred times a day now. Give me your watch. I want to see how it looks on it."

Instead of obeying, Jim tumbled down on the couch and put his hands under the back of his head and smiled.

"Dell," said he, "let's put our Christmas presents away and keep 'em a while. They're too nice to use just at present. I sold the watch to get the money to buy your combs. And now suppose you put the chops on."

The magi, as you know, were wise men—wonderfully wise men—who brought gifts to the Babe in the manger. They invented the art of giving Christmas presents. Being wise, their gifts were no doubt wise ones, possibly bearing the privilege of exchange in case of duplication. And here I have lamely related to you the uneventful chronicle of two foolish children in a flat who most unwisely sacrificed for each other the greatest treasures of their house. But in a last word to the wise of these days let it be said that of all who give gifts these two were the wisest. Of all who give and receive gifts, such as they are wisest. Everywhere they are wisest. They are the magi.

The First Noël

The first Noël, the angel did say,
Was to certain poor shepherds in fields as they lay;
In fields where they lay keeping their sheep,
On a cold winter's night that was so deep.

Chorus
Noël, Noël, Noël, Noël;
Born is the King of Israel!

They looked up and saw a star,
Shining in the East, beyond them far;
And to the earth it gave great light,
And so it continued both day and night.
Chorus

And by the light of that same star,
Three wise men came from country far;
To seek for a King was their intent,
And to follow the star wherever it went.
Chorus

This star drew nigh to the northwest,
O'er Bethlehem it took its rest;
And there it did both stop and stay,
Right over the place where Jesus lay.
Chorus

Then entered in those wise men three,
Full reverently upon their knee;
And offered there in His presence,
Their gold and myrrh and frankincense.
Chorus

Then let us all with one accord,
Sing praises to our heavenly Lord,
Who hath made heaven and earth of nought,
And with His blood mankind hath bought.
Chorus

TRADITIONAL CAROL

Away in a Manger

Away in a manger, no crib for a bed,
The little Lord Jesus laid down his sweet head.
The stars in the sky looked down where he lay,
The little Lord Jesus asleep in the hay.

The cattle are lowing, the baby awakes,
But little Lord Jesus no crying he makes.
I love Thee, Lord Jesus, look down from the sky
And stay by my side 'til morning is nigh.

Be near me, Lord Jesus, I ask Thee to stay
Close by me forever, and love me, I pray.
Bless all the dear children in thy tender care,
And fit us for heaven, to live with Thee there.

GERMAN CAROL

The Fir-Tree

HANS CHRISTIAN ANDERSEN

Far down in the forest, where the warm sun and the fresh air made a sweet resting-place, grew a pretty little fir-tree; and yet it was not happy, it wished so much to be tall like its companions—the pines and firs which grew around it. The sun shone, and the soft air fluttered its leaves, and the little peasant children passed by, prattling merrily, but the fir-tree heeded them not. Sometimes the children would bring a large basket of raspberries or strawberries, wreathed on a straw, and seat themselves near the fir-tree, and say, "Is it not a pretty little tree?" which made it feel more unhappy than before. And yet all this while the tree grew a notch or joint taller every year; for by the number of joints in the stem of a fir-tree we can discover its age. Still, as it grew, it complained, "Oh! how I wish I were as tall as the other trees, then I would spread out my branches on every side, and my top would overlook the wide world. I should have the birds building their nests on my boughs, and when the wind blew, I should bow with stately dignity like my tall companions." The tree was so discontented, that it took no pleasure in the warm sunshine, the birds, or the rosy clouds that floated over it morning and evening. Sometimes, in winter, when the snow lay white and glittering on the ground, a hare would come springing along, and jump right over the little tree; and then how mortified it would feel! Two winters passed, and when the third arrived, the tree had grown so tall that the hare was obliged to run round it. Yet it remained unsatisfied, and would exclaim, "Oh, if I could but keep on growing tall and old! There is nothing else worth caring for in the world!" In the autumn, as usual, the woodcutters came and cut down several of the tallest trees, and the young fir-tree, which was now grown to its full height, shuddered as the noble trees fell to the earth with a crash. After the branches were lopped off, the trunks looked so slender and bare, that they could scarcely be recognised. Then they were placed upon waggons, and drawn by horses out of the forest. "Where were they going? What would become of them?" The young fir-tree wished very much to know; so in the spring, when the swallows and the storks came, it asked, "Do you know where those trees were taken? Did you meet them?"

The swallows knew nothing; but the stork, after a little reflection, nodded his head, and said, "Yes, I think I do. I met several new ships when I flew from Egypt, and they had fine masts that smelt like fir. I think these must have been the trees; I assure you they were stately, very stately."

"Oh, how I wish I were tall enough to go on the sea!" said the fir-tree. "What is this sea, and what does it look like?"

"It would take too much time to explain," said the stork, flying quickly away.

"Rejoice in thy youth," said the sunbeam; "rejoice in thy fresh growth, and the young life that is in thee."

And the wind kissed the tree, and the dew watered it with tears; but the fir-tree regarded them not.

Christmas-time drew near, and many young trees were cut down, some even smaller and younger than the fir-tree who enjoyed neither rest nor peace with longing to leave its forest home. These young trees, which were chosen for their beauty, kept their branches, and were also laid on waggons and drawn by horses out of the forest.

"Where are they going?" asked the fir-tree. "They are not taller than I am: indeed, one is much less; and why are the branches not cut off? Where are they going?"

"We know, we know," sang the sparrows; "we have looked in at the windows of the houses in the town, and we know what is done with them. They are dressed up in the most splendid manner. We have seen them standing in the middle of a warm room, and adorned with all sorts of beautiful things—honey cakes, gilded apples, playthings, and many hundreds of wax tapers."

"And then," asked the fir-tree, trembling through all its branches, "and then what happens?"

"We did not see any more," said the sparrows: "but this was enough for us."

"I wonder whether anything so brilliant will ever happen to me," thought the fir-tree. "It would be much better than crossing the sea. I long for it almost with pain. Oh! When will Christmas be here? I am now as tall and well grown as those which were taken away last year. Oh! That I were now laid on the waggon, or standing in the warm room, with all that brightness and splendour around me! Something better and more beautiful is to come after, or the trees would not be so decked out. Yes, what follows will be grander and more splendid. What can it be? I am weary with longing. I scarcely know how I feel."

"Rejoice with us," said the air and the sunlight. "Enjoy thine own bright life in the fresh air."

But the tree would not rejoice, though it grew taller every day; and, winter and summer, its dark-green foliage might be seen in the forest, while passers-by would say, "What a beautiful tree!"

A short time before Christmas, the discontented fir-tree was the first to fall. As the axe cut through the stem, and divided the pith, the tree fell with a groan to the earth, conscious of pain and faintness, and forgetting all its anticipations of happiness, in sorrow at leaving its home in the forest. It knew that it should never again see its dear old companions, the trees, nor the little bushes and many-coloured flowers that had grown by its side; perhaps not even the birds. Neither was the journey at all pleasant. The tree first recovered itself while being unpacked in the courtyard of a house, with several other trees; and it heard a man say, "We only want one, and this is the prettiest."

Then came two servants in grand livery, and carried the fir-tree into a large and beautiful apartment. On the walls hung pictures, and near the great stove stood great china vases, with lions on the lids. There were rocking-chairs, silken sofas, large tables, covered with pictures, books, and playthings, worth a great deal of money—at least, the children said so. Then the fir-tree was placed in a large tub, full of sand; but green baize hung all round it, so that no one could see it was a tub, and it stood on a very handsome carpet. How the fir-tree trembled! What was going to happen to him now? Some young ladies came, and the servants helped them to adorn the tree. On one branch they hung little bags cut out of coloured paper, and each bag was filled with sweetmeats; from other branches hung gilded apples and walnuts, as if they had grown there; and above, and all round, were hundreds of red, blue, and white tapers, which were fastened on the branches. Dolls, exactly like real babies, were placed under the green leaves—the tree had never seen such things before—and at the very top was fastened a glittering star, made of tinsel. Oh, it was very beautiful!

"This evening," they all exclaimed, "how bright it will be!" "Oh, that the evening were come," thought the tree, "and the tapers lighted! then I shall know what else is going to happen. Will the trees of the forest come to see me? I wonder if the sparrows will peep in at the windows as they fly? Shall I grow faster here, and keep on all these ornaments during summer and winter?" But guessing was of very little use; it made his bark ache, and this pain is as bad for a slender fir-tree, as headache is for us. At last the tapers were lighted, and then what a glistening blaze of light the tree presented! It trembled so with joy in all its branches, that one of the candles fell among the green leaves and burnt some of them. "Help! Help!" exclaimed the young ladies, but there was no danger, for they quickly extinguished the fire. After this, the tree tried not to tremble at all, though the fire frightened him; he was anxious not to hurt any of the beautiful ornaments, even while their brilliancy dazzled him. And now the folding doors were thrown open, and a troop of children rushed in as if they intended to upset the tree; they were followed more slowly by their elders. For a moment the little ones stood silent with astonishment, and then they shouted for joy, till the room rang, and they danced merrily round the tree, while one present after another was taken from it.

"What are they doing? What will happen next?" thought the fir. At last the candles burnt down to the branches, and were put out. Then the children received permission to plunder the tree.

Oh, how they rushed upon it, till the branches cracked, and had it not been fastened with the glistening star to the ceiling, it must have been thrown down. The children then danced about with their pretty toys, and no one noticed the tree, except the children's maid, who came and peeped among the branches to see if an apple or a fig had been forgotten.

"A story, a story," cried the children, pulling a little fat man towards the tree.

"Now we shall be in the green shade," said the man, as he seated himself under it, "and the tree will have the pleasure of hearing also, but I shall only relate one story; what shall it be? 'Ivede-Avede,' or 'Humpty Dumpty,' who fell downstairs, but soon got up again, and at last married a princess."

" 'Ivede-Avede,' " cried some. " 'Humpty Dumpty,' " cried others, and there was a fine shouting and crying out. But the fir-tree remained quite still, and thought to himself, "Shall I have anything to do with all this?" but he had already amused them as much as they wished. Then the old man told them the story of "Humpty Dumpty," how he fell downstairs, and was raised up again, and married a princess. And the children clapped their hands, and cried, "Tell another, tell another," for they wanted to hear the story of "Ivede-Avede"; but they only had "Humpty Dumpty." After this the fir-tree became quite silent and thoughtful; never had the birds in the forest told such tales as "Humpty Dumpty," who fell downstairs, and yet married a princess.

"Ah! yes, so it happens in the world," thought the fir-tree; he believed it all, because it was related by such a nice man. "Ah! well," he thought, "who knows? Perhaps I may fall down too, and marry a princess"; and he looked forward joyfully to the next evening, expecting to be again decked out with lights and playthings, gold and fruit. "To-morrow I will not tremble," thought he; "I will enjoy all my splendour, and I shall hear the story of 'Humpty Dumpty' again, and perhaps 'Ivede-Avede.' " And the tree remained quiet and thoughtful all night. In the morning the servants and the housemaid came in. "Now," thought the fir, "all my splendour is going to begin again." But they dragged him out of the room and upstairs to the garret, and threw him on the floor, in a dark corner, where no daylight shone, and there they left him. "What does this mean?" thought the tree, "What am I to do here? I can hear nothing in a place like this," and he leant against the wall, and thought and thought. And he had time enough to think, for days and nights passed and no one came near him, and when at last somebody did come, it was only to put away large boxes in a corner. So the tree was completely hidden from sight as if it had never existed. "It is winter now," thought the tree, "the ground is hard and covered with snow, so that people cannot plant me. I shall be sheltered here, I dare say, until spring comes. How thoughtful and kind everybody is to me! Still I wish this place were not so dark, as well as lonely, with not even a little hare to look at. How pleasant it was out in the forest while the snow lay on the ground, when the hare would run by, yes, and jump over me too, although I did not like it then. Oh! it is terribly lonely here."

"Squeak, squeak," said a little mouse, creeping cautiously towards the tree; then came another, and they both sniffed at the fir-tree and crept between the branches.

"Oh, it is very cold," said the little mouse, "or else we should be so comfortable here, shouldn't we, you old fir-tree?"

"I am not old," said the fir-tree; "there are many who are older than I am."

"Where do you come from? And what do you know?" asked the mice, who were full of curiosity. "Have you seen the most beautiful places in the world, and can you tell us all about them? And have you been in the storeroom, where cheeses lie on the shelf, and hams hang from the ceiling? One can run about on tallow candles there, and go in thin and come out fat."

"I know nothing of that place," said the fir-tree, "but I know the wood where the sun shines and the birds sing." And then the tree told the little mice all about its youth. They had never heard such an account in their lives; and after they had listened to it attentively, they said, "What a number of things you have seen! You must have been very happy."

"Happy!" exclaimed the fir-tree, and then as he reflected upon what he had been telling them, he said, "Ah, yes! after all, those were happy days." But when he went on and related all about Christmas-eve, and how he had been dressed up with cakes and lights, the mice said, "How happy you must have been, you old fir-tree!"

"I am not old at all," replied the tree, "I only came from the forest this winter; I am not checked in my growth."

"What splendid stories you can relate!" said the little mice. And the next night four other mice came with them to hear what the tree had to tell. The more he talked the more he remembered, and then he thought to himself, "Those were happy days, but they may come again. Humpty Dumpty fell downstairs, and yet he married the princess; perhaps I may marry a princess too." And the fir-tree thought of the pretty little birch-tree that grew in the forest, which was to him a real beautiful princess.

"Who is Humpty Dumpty?" asked the little mice. And then the tree related the whole story; he could remember every single word, and the little mice were so delighted with it, that they were ready to jump to the top of the tree. The next night a great many more mice made their appearance, and on Sunday two rats came with them; but they said, it was not a pretty story at all, and the little mice were very sorry, for it made them also think less of it.

"Do you know only one story?" asked the rats.

"Only one," replied the fir-tree; "I heard it on the happiest evening in my life; but I did not know I was so happy at the time."

"We think it is a very miserable story," said the rats. "Don't you know any story about bacon, or tallow in the storeroom?"

"No," replied the tree.

"Many thanks to you then," replied the rats, and they marched off.

The little mice also kept away after this, and the tree sighed, and said, "It was very pleasant when the merry little mice sat round me and listened while I talked. Now that is all past too. However, I shall consider myself happy when someone comes to take me out of this place." But would this ever happen? Yes; one morning people came to clear out the garret, the boxes were packed away, and the tree was pulled out of the corner, and thrown roughly on the garret floor; then the servant dragged it out upon the staircase where the daylight shone. "Now life is beginning again," said the tree, rejoicing in the sunshine and fresh air. Then it was carried downstairs and taken into the courtyard so quickly, that it forgot to think of itself, and could only look about, there was so much to be seen. The court was close to a garden, where everything looked blooming. Fresh and fragrant roses hung over the little palings. The linden-trees were in blossom; while the swallows flew here and there, crying, "Twit, twit, twit, my mate is coming"—but it was not the fir-tree they meant. "Now I shall live," cried the tree, joyfully spreading out its branches; but alas! they were all withered and yellow, and it lay in a corner amongst weeds and nettles. The star of gold paper still stuck in the top of the tree and glittered in the sunshine. In the same courtyard two of the merry children were playing who had danced round the tree at Christmas, and had been so happy. The youngest saw the gilded star, and ran and pulled it off the tree. "Look what is sticking to the ugly old fir-tree," said the child, treading on the branches till they crackled under his boots. And the tree saw all the fresh bright flowers in the garden, and then looked at itself, and wished it remained in the dark corner of the garret. It thought of its fresh youth in the forest, of the merry Christmas evening, and of the little mice who had listened to the story of "Humpty Dumpty." "Past! past!" said the old tree. "Oh, had I but enjoyed myself while I could have done so! But now it is too late." Then a lad came and chopped the tree into small pieces, till a large bundle lay in a heap on the ground. The pieces were placed in a fire under the copper, and they quickly blazed up brightly, while the tree sighed so deeply that each sigh was like a little pistol-shot. Then the children, who were at play, came and seated themselves in front of the fire, and looked at it, and cried, "Pop, pop." But at each "pop," which was a deep sigh, the tree was thinking of a summer day in the forest, or of some winter night there, when the stars shone brightly; and of Christmas evening, and of "Humpty Dumpty," the only story it had ever heard or knew how to relate, till at last it was consumed. The boys still played in the garden, and the youngest wore the golden star on his breast, with which the tree had been adorned during the happiest evening of its existence. Now all was past; the tree's life was past, and the story also—for all stories must come to an end at last.

O Christmas Tree

(O Tannenbaum)

O Christmas tree, O Christmas tree,
With faithful leaves unchanging.
Not only green in summer's heat,
But also winter's snow and sleet.
O Christmas tree, O Christmas tree,
With faithful leaves unchanging.

O Christmas tree, O Christmas tree,
Of all the trees most lovely;
Each year, you bring to me delight
Gleaming in the Christmas night.
O Christmas tree, O Christmas tree,
Of all the trees most lovely.

O Christmas tree, O Christmas tree,
Your leaves will teach me, also,
That hope and love and faithfulness
Are precious things I can possess.
O Christmas tree, O Christmas tree,
Your leaves will teach me, also.

GERMAN CAROL

Christmas Trees

A Christmas Circular Letter

The city had withdrawn into itself
And left at last the country to the country;
When between whirls of snow not come to lie
And whirls of foliage not yet laid, there drove
A stranger to our yard, who looked the city,
Yet did in country fashion in that there
He sat and waited till he drew us out
A-buttoning coats to ask him who he was.
He proved to be the city come again
To look for something it had left behind
And could not do without and keep its Christmas.
He asked if I would sell my Christmas trees;
My woods—the young fir balsams like a place
Where houses all are churches and have spires.
I hadn't thought of them as Christmas trees.
I doubt if I was tempted for a moment
To sell them off their feet to go in cars
And leave the slope behind the house all bare,
Where the sun shines now no warmer than the moon.
I'd hate to have them know it if I was.
Yet more I'd hate to hold my trees except
As others hold theirs or refuse for them,
Beyond the time of profitable growth,
The trail by market everything must come to.
I dallied so much with the thought of selling.

Then whether from mistaken courtesy
And fear of seeming short of speech, or whether
From hope of hearing good of what was mine,
I said, 'There aren't enough to be worth while.'

'I could soon tell how many they would cut,
You let me look them over.'

'You could look.
But don't expect I'm going to let you have them.'
Pasture they spring in, some in clumps too close
That lop each other of boughs, but not a few
Quite solitary and having equal boughs
All round and round. The latter he nodded 'Yes' to,
Or paused to say beneath some lovelier one,
With a buyer's moderation, 'That would do.'
I thought so too, but wasn't there to say so.
We climbed the pasture on the south, crossed over,
And came down on the north.

He said, 'A thousand.'

'A thousand Christmas trees!—at what apiece?'

He felt some need of softening that to me:
'A thousand trees would come to thirty dollars.'
Then I was certain I had never meant
To let him have them. Never show surprise!
But thirty dollars seemed so small beside

The extent of pasture I should strip, three cents
(For that was all they figured out apiece),
Three cents so small beside the dollar friends
I should be writing to within the hour
Would pay in cities for good trees like those,
Regular vestry-trees whole Sunday Schools
Could hang enough on to pick off enough.
A thousand Christmas trees I didn't know I had!
Worth three cents more to give away than sell,
As may be shown by a simple calculation.
Too bad I couldn't lay one in a letter.
I can't help wishing I could send you one,
In wishing you herewith a Merry Christmas.

ROBERT FROST

A Visit from St. Nicholas

'Twas the night before Christmas, when all through
the house
Not a creature was stirring, not even a mouse;
The stockings were hung by the chimney with care,
In hopes that St. Nicholas soon would be there.
The children were nestled all snug in their beds,
While visions of sugar-plums danced through
their heads;
And mamma in her kerchief, and I in my cap,
Had just settled our brains for a long winter's nap—
When out on the lawn there arose such a clatter,
I sprang from my bed to see what was the matter.
Away to the window I flew like a flash,
Tore open the shutters and threw up the sash.
The moon on the breast of the new-fallen snow
Gave the lustre of midday to objects below;
When, what to my wondering eyes should appear,
But a miniature sleigh and eight tiny reindeer,
With a little old driver, so lively and quick,
I knew in a moment it must be St. Nick.
More rapid than eagles his coursers they came,
And he whistled, and shouted, and called them
by name:
"Now, Dasher! now, Dancer! now, Prancer!
and Vixen!
On, Comet! on, Cupid! on, Donder and Blitzen!

To the top of the porch! to the top of the wall!
Now dash away! dash away! dash away all!"
As dry leaves that before the wild hurricane fly,
When they meet with an obstacle, mount to the sky,
So up to the house-top the coursers they flew,
With the sleighful of toys, and St. Nicholas too.
And then in a twinkling I heard on the roof
The prancing and pawing of each little hoof.
As I drew in my head, and was turning around,
Down the chimney St. Nicholas came with a bound.
He was dressed all in fur from his head to his foot,
And his clothes were all tarnished with ashes and soot;
A bundle of toys he had flung on his back,
And he looked like a peddlar just opening his pack.
His eyes, how they twinkled! his dimples, how merry!
His cheeks were like roses, his nose like a cherry!
His droll little mouth was drawn up like a bow,
And the beard on his chin was as white as the snow.
The stump of a pipe he held tight in his teeth,
And the smoke, it encircled his head like a wreath.
He had a broad face, and a little round belly
That shook, when he laughed, like a bowl full of jelly.
He was chubby and plump—a right jolly old elf;
And I laughed, when I saw him, in spite of myself.
A wink of his eye, and a twist of his head
Soon gave me to know I had nothing to dread.
He spoke not a word, but went straight to his work,
And filled all the stockings; then turned with a jerk,
And laying his finger aside of his nose,

And giving a nod, up the chimney he rose.
He sprang to his sleigh, to the team gave a whistle,
And away they all flew, like the down of a thistle,
But I heard him exclaim, ere he drove out of sight,
"Happy Christmas to all, and to all a good-night!"

CLEMENT CLARKE MOORE

Jingle Bells

Dashing thro' the snow in a one-horse open sleigh,
O'er the fields we go, laughing all the way;
Bells on bob-tail ring, making spirits bright;
What fun it is to ride and sing a sleighing song tonight!

Chorus
Jingle bells! Jingle bells! Jingle all the way!
Oh! what fun it is to ride in a one-horse open sleigh!

A day or two ago I thought I'd take a ride,
And soon Miss Fanny Bright was seated by my side;
The horse was lean and lank, misfortunes seemed his lot,
He got into a drifted bank, and we got upsot.
Chorus

Now the ground is white, go it while you're young,
Take the girls tonight, and sing this sleighing song;
Just get a bob-tailed nag, two-forty for his speed,
Then hitch him to an open sleigh, and crack! you'll take the lead.
Chorus

J. PIERPONT

Yes, Virginia, There Is a Santa Claus

FRANCIS P. CHURCH

In 1897, eight-year-old Virginia O'Hanlon wrote a letter to The New York Sun *with an earnest question about the existence of Santa Claus. The letter wound up in the hands of Francis P. Church, a veteran editor who had covered the Civil War for* The New York Times *and who had worked at* The Sun *for twenty years. A tough journalist known for his commentary on controversial subjects, Church answered the little girl. His response, which appeared on the paper's editorial page on September 21, 1897, became an instant classic and was reprinted every year in* The Sun *until the paper went out of business in 1949.*

We take pleasure in answering thus prominently the communication below, expressing at the same time our great gratification that its faithful author is numbered among the friends of *The Sun:*

Dear Editor:
I am 8 years old. Some of my little friends say there is no Santa Claus. Papa says, "If you see it in The Sun, *it's so."*
Please tell me the truth, is there a Santa Claus?
Virginia O'Hanlon
115 West 95th Street

Virginia, your little friends are wrong. They have been affected by the scepticism of a sceptical age. They do not believe except they see. They think that nothing can be which is not comprehensible by their little minds. All minds, Virginia, whether they be men's or children's, are little. In this great universe of ours, man is a mere insect, an ant, in his intellect as compared with the boundless world about him, as measured by the intelligence capable of grasping the whole of truth and knowledge.

Yes, Virginia, there is a Santa Claus. He exists as certainly as love and generosity and devotion exist, and you know that they abound and give to your life its highest beauty and joy. Alas! how dreary would be the world if there were no Santa Claus! It would be as dreary as if there were no Virginias. There would be no childlike faith then, no poetry, no romance to make tolerable this existence. We should have no enjoyment, except in sense and sight. The external light with which childhood fills the world would be extinguished.

Not believe in Santa Claus! You might as well not believe in fairies. You might get your papa to hire men to watch in all the chimneys on Christmas eve to catch Santa Claus, but even if you did not see Santa Claus coming down, what would that prove? Nobody sees Santa Claus, but that is no sign that there is no Santa Claus. The most real things in the world are those that neither children nor men can see. Did you ever see fairies dancing on the lawn? Of course not, but that's no proof that they are not there. Nobody can conceive or imagine all the wonders there are unseen and unseeable in the world.

You tear apart the baby's rattle and see what makes the noise inside, but there is a veil covering the unseen world which not the strongest man, nor even the united strength of all the strongest men that ever lived could tear apart. Only faith, poetry, love, romance, can push aside that curtain and view and picture the supernal beauty and glory beyond. Is it all real? Ah, Virginia, in all this world there is nothing else real and abiding.

No Santa Claus! Thank God he lives and lives forever. A thousand years from now, Virginia, nay 10 times 10,000 years from now, he will continue to make glad the heart of childhood.

Gift Rap

TERRY KAY

The best memory I have of Christmas, as a parent, was the evening that my oldest daughter—then a one-year-old—pulled a wrapped package beneath the tree two days earlier than Santa Claus would have liked, and proceeded to rip it open.

Inside the package was a doll, a squint-eyed thing that I considered on-purpose, new-born-baby ugly. I had protested to my wife that it would cause nightmares or even more severe traumas. My complaints were ignored with a stare that said, "This is a mother-daughter thing."

Of course, she was right. My daughter's face was radiant when she tore open the box.

"Baby," she whispered in awe. "Baby." She held it to her face, like a mother being tender with her child.

That doll became Lucy, and from that Christmas until

she was lost on a trip many years later, Lucy was always within reach of my daughter. The tears of woe over that sad mishap were so great, I have spent almost thirty years trying to duplicate Lucy in flea markets and doll shops.

My daughter had cried, "There's only one Lucy."

After all these years, I believe her.

Point is, shopping for Christmas toys is not an easy task, especially today.

The choices are too many, too appealing.

Used to be—or so memory tells me—it was as simple as a walk-through in a five-and-dime store.

Boys got something from the sports table, or toy pistols, or toy cars. Maybe some Tinker-toys, or pick-up sticks. Maybe even a Red Ryder BB rifle.

Girls got dolls, and other stuff. I don't know what, make-believe makeup kits, maybe. Imitation jewelry. I didn't pay very much attention.

No one fretted that what was being given would be sneered at, or refused, or ignored. A gift was something, and something was considerably better than nothing.

Not so today.

Today, everyone seems to want a toy that is popular, safe, educational, durable, relatively inexpensive, and one that ranks high on the Child Delight Meter.

The only thing I know that comes close to meeting the above requisites is a large cardboard shipping box:

Popular—How many of us have watched children tear open a gift, turn it over a couple of times, toss it away, and pick up the box it came in?

Safe—Sure, youngsters can get hurt playing with, or in, boxes, but chances are the toy inside the box is far more dangerous.

Educational—With boxes, children must use their imagination. Does a greater instrument of education exist than the imagination?

Durable—Boxes are like good dogs around children. They can take the punishment and still be there.

Relatively inexpensive—How much can a box cost in comparison to the gift it holds?

Child Delight Meter—refer to "popular" and "educational" items above, or better yet, refer to experience.

In addition, a box does not require batteries, which are never included when they should be included. It does not need late-night home assembly with directions that not even the CIA could follow. It can be drawn on with Magic Marker and become magical. And when it is finally crushed from the weight of imagination—from being submarines and spaceships, dollhouses and dark caves—it may be recycled for such mundane purposes as holding items for sale. It is even biodegradable for those too casual to recycle.

Yet, to my knowledge, no one makes cardboard shipping boxes for the express purpose of functioning as a toy, and in that decision or oversight is a statement about our values that is worth pondering: If we get a wrapped box, we expect something other than possibility to be inside it.

Still, like most shoppers, I enjoy the annual dilemma of the what and how many of Christmas toys, and then the rushing-around search to find them at a slashed-price deal.

(And I am referring only to children's toys, not that gaudy nonsense annually advertised for over-rich adults. A Mercedes golf cart? May it dogleg left and find the fairway to hell.)

An investigative tour of one of the Toys "R" Us stores is a trip into a latter-day land of fantasy. Little wonder the corporate powers that be are building twenty-five, thirty of these toy-stacked emporiums each year in America. They know that cash flow is bound to follow the squeal of childish joy.

We used to be happy with a simple game of checkers. Now they have a board that can be used for checkers, chess, backgammon, Parcheesi, Chinese checkers, and something called Chutes & Ladders.

The standards are still available, but they're often hard to recognize.

The toy truck we once pushed around in the back yard has now been upgraded by Tonka to the size of a riding lawn mower.

The roller skate is now an in-line skate, or something called a Rollerblade.

You can now buy a kite that looks like a fighter plane and has electronic battling sounds.

And I swear there are bicycles with more gears than spokes in the wheels.

Barbie, the doll's doll, is still as youthful and fetching as Brenda Starr, and still on the shelves, but she's a modern woman of action. She can be found in a Patio Party box, or a Backyard Cookout box, or a Sunshine Holiday box, and a few other places where the energetic gather. She is even featured in a wedding dress, which makes me wonder if she's managed to trap Ken at the altar. Oh, yes, Ken's still around. Still smiling, the little devil that he is. Personally, I think he's got his eye on Midge, Barbie's best friend.

And the Cabbage Patch Kids are plentiful. My favorite is the one called Newborn (but it's not Lucy). It is advertised with a "magical monitor," and it "cries, giggles, and calls 'Ma Ma.' " Cute, real cute.

But there always seems to be a head-liner Christmas gift, and, if the pleading of my oldest grandson—son of Lucy's mother—is an indicator, that gift would have to be from Nintendo.

The Nintendo games are advertised as the World of Nintendo. There's no brag in the claim. It is a world. Strange. Baffling. And every year, something new.

That, of course, is the key to toy manufacturing: Keep it coming with upgraded and improved product. The new look, the new appeal. It's a little like adults who collect Christmas plates from Hummel. If it's another year, there's another edition.

According to Matt Dodge, the assistant inventory control manager for the Southeast region of Toys "R" Us, the key to the business of toys is ". . . always to keep fresh."

Dodge admits that even Nintendo has leveled off over the years, but, ". . . they keep bringing out new generations of software, offering new and more exciting games."

Dodge must be right. My grandson tells me the same thing, insisting that he will be considered the neighborhood oddball if he can't have his fingers flying over the latest Nintendo challenge.

He thinks I am a sucker for his woeful expression. He is right.

But all of this is the *business* of toys, which doesn't necessarily have anything to do with the *spirit* of toys. The spirit touches the heart, not the wallet.

In his book *Without Reservations,* Fred Alias presents a story about a hotel clerk who was shopping one day in a thrift store and overheard a small girl begging her mother for a doll's house that was in need of repair. The mother tried to explain that there was no money for dollhouses, that a winter coat was more important.

The hotel clerk followed the mother and child when they left the store, noting their address. He then went back to the thrift shop, purchased the dollhouse, and spent his spare time repairing it. On Christmas Eve, he tied a bow around the dollhouse and delivered it in the middle of the night to the front steps of the home where the girl lived.

Forgive me for being sentimental, but I like that story. It reminds that there are things that can't be purchased in Toys "R" Us, or any other shop.

And I think it confirms something that's important at Christmas: A doll's house given out of caring is more valuable than diamonds—if your heart is the heart of a child. If it isn't, you will never understand what giving, or receiving, really means, anyway.

My Father's Telescope

The oldest joke
in the world,
a chair on three legs.

Sawdust kicks
up, swirls
around his boots

and settles
in the cuffs of his
pants. The saw is

as nervous as
a parrot.
The chair

shrinks. After
years of cupboards
and end tables, after

a plywood Santa
and seven elves
for the lawn in snow,

he knows.
He's failed, and
in oak.

Next Christmas
he buys himself
and his son

a telescope.

RITA DOVE

Christmas Day in the Morning

PEARL S. BUCK

He woke suddenly and completely. It was four o'clock, the hour at which his father had always called him to get up and help with the milking. Strange how the habits of his youth clung to him still! Fifty years ago, and his father had been dead for thirty years, and yet he woke at four o'clock, in the morning. He had trained himself to turn over and go to sleep, but this morning, because it was Christmas, he did not try to sleep.

Yet what was the magic of Christmas now? His childhood and youth were long past, and his own children had grown up and gone. Some of them lived only a few miles away, but they had their own families, and they would come in as usual toward the end of the day. They had explained with infinite gentleness that they wanted their children to build Christmas memories about their houses, not his. He was left alone with his wife.

Yesterday she had said, "It isn't worthwhile, perhaps—"

And he had said, "Oh, yes, Alice, even if there are only the two of us, let's have a Christmas of our own."

Then she had said, "Let's not trim the tree until tomorrow, Robert. Just so it's ready when the children come. I'm tired."

He had agreed, and the tree was still out in the back entry.

He lay in his big bed in his room. The door to her room was shut, because she was a light sleeper and sometimes he had restless nights. Years ago they had decided to use separate rooms. It meant nothing, they said, except that neither of them slept as well as they once had. They had been married so long that nothing could separate them, actually.

Why did he feel so awake tonight? For it was still night, a clear and starry night. No moon, of course, but the stars were extraordinary! Now that he thought of it, the stars seemed always large and clear before the dawn of Christmas Day. There was one star now that was certainly larger and brighter than any of the others. He could even imagine it moving, as it had seemed to him to move one night long ago.

He slipped back in time, as he did so easily nowadays. He was fifteen years old and still on his father's farm. He loved his father. He had not known it until one time a few days before Christmas, when he had overheard what his father was saying to his mother.

"Mary, I hate to call Rob in the mornings. He's growing so fast and he needs his sleep. If you could see how he sleeps when I go in to wake him up! I wish I could manage alone."

"Well, you can't, Adam." His mother's voice was brisk. "Besides, he isn't a child anymore. It's time he took his turn."

"Yes," his father said slowly. "But I sure do hate to wake him."

When he heard these words, something in him woke. His father loved him! He had never thought of it before, taking for granted the tie of their blood. Neither his father nor his mother talked about their children; they had no time for such things. There was always so much to do on a farm.

Now he knew his father loved him, there would be no more loitering in the mornings and having to be called again. He got up after that, stumbling blind with sleep, and pulled on his clothes, his eyes tight shut, but he got up.

And then on the night before Christmas, that year when he was fifteen, he lay for a few minutes thinking about the next day. They were poor, and most of the excitement was in the turkey they had raised themselves and in the mince pies his mother made. His sisters sewed presents, and his mother and father always bought something he needed, not only a warm jacket, maybe, but something more, such as a book. And he saved and bought them each something too.

He wished, that Christmas he was fifteen, he had a better present for his father. As usual he had gone to the ten-cent store and bought a tie. It had seemed nice enough until he lay thinking the night before Christmas, and then he wished that he had heard his father and mother talking in time for him to save for something better.

He lay on his side, his head supported by his elbow, and looked out his attic window. The stars were bright, much brighter than he ever remembered seeing them, and one star in particular was so bright that he wondered if it were really the Star of Bethlehem.

"Dad," he had once asked, when he was a little boy, "what is a stable?"

"It's just a barn," his father had replied, "like ours."

Then Jesus had been born in a barn, and to a barn the shepherds and the Wise Men had come, bringing their Christmas gifts!

The thought had struck him like a silver dagger. Why should he not give his father a special gift too, out there in the barn? He could get up early, earlier than four o'clock, and he could creep into the barn and get all the milking done. He'd do it alone, milk and clean up, and then when his father went in to start the milking he'd see it all done. And he could know who had done it.

He laughed to himself as he gazed at the stars. It was what he would do, and he mustn't sleep too sound.

He must have waked twenty times, scratching a match each time to look at his old watch— midnight, and half past one, and then two o'clock.

At a quarter to three he got up and put on his clothes. He crept downstairs, careful of the creaky boards, and let himself out. The big star hung lower over the barn roof, a reddish gold. The cows looked at him, sleepy and surprised. It was early for them too.

"So, boss," he whispered. They accepted him placidly, and he fetched some hay for each cow, and then got the milking pail and the big milk cans.

He had never milked all alone before, but it seemed almost easy. He kept thinking about his father's surprise. His father would come in and call him, saying that he would get things started while Rob was getting dressed. He'd go to the barn, open the door, and then he'd go to get the two big empty milk cans. But they wouldn't be waiting or empty; they'd be standing in the milkhouse, filled.

"What the—" he could hear his father exclaiming.

He smiled and milked steadily, two strong streams rushing into the pail, frothing and fragrant. The cows were still surprised but acquiescent. For once they were behaving well, as though they knew it was Christmas.

The task went more easily than he had ever known it to before. Milking for once was not a chore. It was something else, a gift to his father, who loved him. He finished, the two milk cans were full, and he covered them and closed the milkhouse door carefully, making sure of the latch. He put the stool in its place by the door and hung up the clean milk pail. Then he went out of the barn and barred the door behind him.

Back in his room he had only a minute to pull off his clothes in the darkness and jump into bed, for he heard his father up. He put the covers over his head to silence his quick breathing. The door opened.

"Rob!" his father called. "We have to get up, son, even if it is Christmas."

"Aw right," he said sleepily.

"I'll go on out," his father said. "I'll get things started." The door closed and he lay still, laughing to himself. In just a few minutes his father would know. His dancing heart was ready to jump from his body.

The minutes were endless—ten, fifteen, he did not know how many—before he heard his father's footsteps again. The door opened and he lay still.

"Rob!"

"Yes, Dad—"

"You son of a—" His father was laughing, a queer, sobbing sort of laugh. "Thought you'd fool me, did you?" His father was standing beside his bed, feeling for him, pulling away the cover.

"It's for Christmas, Dad!"

He found his father and clutched him in a great hug. He felt his father's arms go around him. It was dark and they could not see each other's faces.

"Son, I thank you. Nobody ever did a nicer thing—"

"Oh, Dad, I want you to know—I do want to be good!" The words broke from him of their own will. He did not know what to say. His heart was bursting with love.

"Well, I reckon I can go back to bed and sleep," his father said after a moment. "No, hark, the little ones are waked up. Come to think of it, son, I've never seen you children when you first saw the Christmas tree. I was always in the barn. Come on!"

He got up and pulled on his clothes again, and they went down to the Christmas tree, and soon the sun was creeping up to where the star had been. Oh, what a Christmas, and how his heart had nearly burst again with shyness and pride as his father told his mother and made the younger children listen about how he, Rob, had got up all by himself.

"The best Christmas gift I ever had, and I'll remember it, son, every year on Christmas morning, so long as I live."

They had both remembered it, and now that his father was dead he remembered it alone, that blessed Christmas dawn when, alone with the cows in the barn, he had made his first gift of true love.

Outside the window now the great star slowly sank. He got up out of bed and put on his slippers and bathrobe and went softly upstairs to the attic and found the box of Christmas-tree decorations. He took them downstairs into the living room. Then he brought in the tree. It was a little one—they had not had a big tree since the children went away—but he set it in the holder and put it in the middle of the long table under the window. Then carefully he began to trim it.

It was done very soon, the time passing as quickly as it had that morning long ago in the barn. He went to his library and fetched the little box that contained his special gift to his wife, a star of diamonds, not large but dainty in design. He had written the card for it the day before. He tied the gift on the tree and then stood back. It was pretty, very pretty, and she would be surprised.

But he was not satisfied. He wanted to tell her, to tell

her how much he loved her. It had been a long time since he had really told her, although he loved her in a very special way, much more than he ever had when they were young.

He had been fortunate that she had loved him, and how fortunate that he had been able to love! Ah, that was the true joy of life, the ability to love! For he was quite sure that some people were genuinely unable to love anyone. But love was alive in him; it still was.

It occurred to him suddenly that it was alive because long ago it had been born in him when he knew his father loved him. That was it: love alone could waken love.

And he could give the gift again and again. This morning, this blessed Christmas morning, he would give it to his beloved wife. He could write it down in a letter for her to read and keep forever. He went to his desk and began his love letter to his wife: "My dearest love. . . ."

When it was finished he sealed it and tied it on the tree where she would see it the first thing when she came into the room. She would read it, surprised and then moved, and realize how very much he loved her.

He put out the light and went tiptoeing up the stairs. The star in the sky was gone, and the first rays of the sun were gleaming the sky. Such a happy, happy Christmas!

Old Folks' Christmas

RING LARDNER

Tom and Grace Carter sat in their living-room on Christmas Eve, sometimes talking, sometimes pretending to read and all the time thinking things they didn't want to think. Their two children, Junior, aged nineteen, and Grace, two years younger, had come home that day from their schools for the Christmas vacation. Junior was in his first year at the university and Grace attending a boarding-school that would fit her for college.

I won't call them Grace and Junior any more, though that is the way they had been christened. Junior had changed his name to Ted and Grace was now Caroline, and thus they insisted on being addressed, even by their parents. This was one of the things Tom and Grace the elder were thinking of as they sat in their living-room Christmas Eve.

Other university freshmen who had lived here had returned on the twenty-first, the day when the vacation was supposed to begin. Ted had telegraphed that he would be three days late owing to a special examination which, if he passed it, would lighten the terrific burden of the next term. He had arrived at home looking so pale, heavy-eyed and shaky that his mother doubted the wisdom of the concentrated mental effort, while his father secretly hoped the stuff had been non-poisonous and would not have lasting effects. Caroline, too, had been behind schedule, explaining that her laundry had gone astray and she had not dared trust others to trace it for her.

Grace and Tom had attempted, with fair success, to conceal their disappointment over this delayed home-coming and had continued with their preparations for a Christmas that would thrill their children and consequently themselves. They had bought an imposing lot of presents, costing twice or three times as much as had been Tom's father's annual income when Tom was Ted's age, or Tom's own income a year ago, before General Motors' acceptance of his new weather-proof paint had enabled him to buy this suburban home and luxuries such as his own parents and Grace's had never dreamed of, and to give Ted and Caroline advantages that he and Grace had perforce gone without.

Behind the closed door of the music-room was the elaborately decked tree. The piano and piano bench and the floor around the tree were covered with beribboned packages of all sizes, shapes and weights, one of them addressed to Tom, another to Grace, a few to the servants and the rest to Ted and Caroline. A huge box contained a sealskin coat for Caroline, a coat that had cost as much as the Carters had formerly paid a year for rent. Even more expensive was a "set" of jewelry consisting of an opal brooch, a bracelet of opals and gold filigree, and an opal ring surrounded by diamonds.

Grace always had preferred opals to any other stone, but now that she could afford them, some inhibition prevented her from buying them for herself; she could enjoy them much more adorning her pretty daughter. There were boxes of silk stockings, lingerie, gloves and handkerchiefs. And for Ted, a three-hundred-dollar watch, a de-luxe edition of Balzac, an expensive bag of shiny, new steel-shafted golf-clubs and the last word in portable phonographs.

But the big surprise for the boy was locked in the garage, a black Gorham sedan, a model more up to date and better-looking than Tom's own year-old car that stood beside it. Ted could use it during the vacation if the mild weather continued and could look forward to driving it around home next spring and summer, there being a rule at the university forbidding undergraduates the possession or use of private automobiles.

Every year for sixteen years, since Ted was three and Caroline one, it had been the Christmas Eve custom of the Carters to hang up their children's stockings and fill them with inexpensive toys. Tom and Grace had thought it would be fun to continue the custom this year; the contents of the stockings—a mechanical negro dancing doll, music-boxes, a kitten that meowed when you pressed a spot on her back, et cetera—would make the "kids" laugh. And one of Grace's first pronouncements to her returned offspring was that they must go to bed early so Santa Claus would not be frightened away.

But it seemed they couldn't promise to make it so terribly early. They both had long-standing dates in town. Caroline was going to dinner and a play with Beatrice Murdock and Beatrice's nineteen-year-old brother Paul. The latter would call for her in his car at half past six. Ted had accepted an invitation to see the hockey match with two classmates, Herb Castle and Bernard King. He wanted to take his father's Gorham, but Tom told him untruthfully that the foot-brake was not working; Ted must be kept out of the garage till tomorrow morning.

Ted and Caroline had taken naps in the afternoon and gone off together in Paul Murdock's stylish roadster, giving their word that they would be back by midnight or a little later and that tomorrow night they would stay home.

And now their mother and father were sitting up for them, because the stockings could not be filled and hung till they were safely in bed, and also because trying to go to sleep is a painful and hopeless business when you are kind of jumpy.

"What time is it?" asked Grace, looking up from the third page of a book that she had begun to "read" soon after dinner.

"Half past two," said her husband. (He had answered the same question every fifteen or twenty minutes since midnight.)

"You don't suppose anything could have happened?" said Grace.

"We'd have heard if there had," said Tom.

"It isn't likely, of course," said Grace, "but they might have had an accident some place where nobody was there to report it or telephone or anything. We don't know what kind of a driver the Murdock boy is."

"He's Ted's age. Boys that age may be inclined to drive too fast, but they drive pretty well."

"How do you know?"

"Well, I've watched some of them drive."

"Yes, but not all of them."

"I doubt whether anybody in the world has seen every nineteen-year-old boy drive."

"Boys these days seem so kind of irresponsible."

"Oh, don't worry! They probably met some of their young friends and stopped for a bite to eat or something." Tom got up and walked to the window with studied carelessness. "It's a pretty night," he said. "You can see every star in the sky."

But he wasn't looking at the stars. He was looking down the road for headlights. There were none in sight and after a few moments he returned to his chair.

"What time is it?" asked Grace.

"Twenty-two of," he said.

"Of what?"

"Of three."

"Your watch must have stopped. Nearly an hour ago you told me it was half past two."

"My watch is all right. You probably dozed off."

"I haven't closed my eyes."

"Well, it's time you did. Why don't you go to bed?"

"Why don't *you*?"

"I'm not sleepy."

"Neither am I. But honestly, Tom, it's silly for you to stay up. I'm just doing it so I can fix the stockings, and because I feel so wakeful. But there's no use of your losing your sleep."

"I couldn't sleep a wink till they're home."

"That's foolishness! There's nothing to worry about. They're just having a good time. You were young once yourself."

"That's just it! When I was young, I was young." He picked up his paper and tried to get interested in the shipping news.

"What time is it?" asked Grace.

"Five minutes of three."

"Maybe they're staying at the Murdocks' all night."

"They'd have let us know."

"They were afraid to wake us up, telephoning."

At three-twenty a car stopped at the front gate.

"There they are!"

"I told you there was nothing to worry about."

Tom went to the window. He could just discern the outlines of the Murdock boy's roadster, whose lighting system seemed to have broken down.

"He hasn't any lights," said Tom. "Maybe I'd better go out and see if I can fix them."

"No, don't!" said Grace sharply. "He can fix them himself. He's just saving them while he stands still."

"Why don't they come in?"

"They're probably making plans."

"They can make them in here. I'll go out and tell them we're still up."

"No, don't!" said Grace as before, and Tom obediently remained at the window.

It was nearly four when the car lights flashed on and the car drove away. Caroline walked into the house and stared dazedly at her parents.

"Heavens! What are you doing up?"

Tom was about to say something, but Grace forestalled him.

"We were talking over old Christmases," she said. "Is it very late?"

"I haven't any idea," said Caroline.

"Where is Ted?"

"Isn't he home? I haven't seen him since we dropped him at the hockey place."

"Well, you go right to bed," said her mother. "You must be worn out."

"I am, kind of. We danced after the play. What time is breakfast?"

"Eight o'clock."

"Oh, Mother, can't you make it nine?"

"I guess so. You used to want to get up early on Christmas."

"I know, but—"

"Who brought you home?" asked Tom.

"Why, Paul Murdock—and Beatrice."

"You look rumpled."

"They made me sit in the 'rumple' seat."

She laughed at her joke, said good night and went upstairs. She had not come even within hand-shaking distance of her father and mother.

"The Murdocks," said Tom, "must have great manners, making their guest ride in that uncomfortable seat."

Grace was silent.

"You go to bed, too," said Tom. "I'll wait for Ted."

"You couldn't fix the stockings."

"I won't try. We'll have time for that in the morning; I mean, later in the morning."

"I'm not going to bed till you do," said Grace.

"All right, we'll both go. Ted ought not to be long now. I suppose his friends will bring him home. We'll hear him when he comes in."

There was no chance not to hear him when, at ten minutes before six, he came in. He had done his Christmas shopping late and brought home a package.

Grace was downstairs again at half past seven, telling the servants breakfast would be postponed till nine. She nailed the stockings beside the fireplace, went into the music-room to see that nothing had been disturbed and removed Ted's hat and overcoat from where he had carefully hung them on the hall floor.

Tom appeared a little before nine and suggested that the children ought to be awakened.

"I'll wake them," said Grace, and went upstairs. She opened Ted's door, looked, and softly closed it again. She entered her daughter's room and found Caroline semiconscious.

"Do I have to get up now? Honestly I can't eat anything. If you could just have Molla bring me some coffee. Ted and I are both invited to the Murdocks' for breakfast at half past twelve, and I could sleep for another hour or two."

"But dearie, don't you know we have Christmas dinner at one?"

"It's a shame, Mother, but I thought of course our dinner would be at night."

"Don't you want to see your presents?"

"Certainly I do, but can't they wait?"

Grace was about to go to the kitchen to tell the cook that dinner would be at seven instead of one, but she remembered having promised Signe the afternoon and evening off, as a cold, light supper would be all anyone wanted after the heavy midday meal.

Tom and Grace breakfasted alone and once more sat in the living-room, talking, thinking and pretending to read.

"You ought to speak to Caroline," said Tom.

"I will, but not today. It's Christmas."

"And I intend to say a few words to Ted."

"Yes, dear, you must. But not today."

"I suppose they'll be out again tonight."

"No, they promised to stay home. We'll have a nice cozy evening."

"Don't bet too much on that," said Tom.

At noon the "children" made their entrance and responded to their parents' salutations with almost the proper warmth.

Ted declined a cup of coffee and he and Caroline apologized for making a "breakfast" date at the Murdocks'.

"Sis and I both thought you'd be having dinner at seven, as usual."

"We've always had it at one o'clock on Christmas," said Tom.

"I'd forgotten it was Christmas," said Ted.

"Well, those stockings ought to remind you."

Ted and Caroline looked at the bulging stockings.

"Isn't there a tree?" asked Caroline.

"Of course," said her mother. "But the stockings come first."

"We've only a little time," said Caroline. "We'll be terribly late as it is. So can't we see the tree now?"

"I guess so," said Grace, and led the way into the music-room.

The servants were summoned and the tree stared at and admired.

"You must open your presents," said Grace to her daughter.

"I can't open them all now," said Caroline. "Tell me which is special."

The cover was removed from the huge box and Grace held up the coat.

"Oh, Mother!" said Caroline. "A sealskin coat!"

"Put it on," said her father.

"Not now. We haven't time."

"Then look at this!" said Grace, and opened the case of jewels.

"Oh, Mother! Opals!" said Caroline.

"They're my favorite stone," said Grace quietly.

"If nobody minds," said Ted, "I'll postpone my personal investigation till we get back. I know I'll like everything you've given me. But if we have no car in working order, I've got to call a taxi and catch a train."

"You can drive in," said his father.

"Did you fix the brake?"

"I think it's all right. Come up to the garage and we'll see."

Ted got his hat and coat and kissed his mother good-by.

"Mother," he said, "I know you'll forgive me for not having any presents for you and Dad. I was so rushed the last three days at school. And I thought I'd have time to shop a little when we got in yesterday, but I was in too much of a hurry to be home. Last night, everything was closed."

"Don't worry," said Grace. "Christmas is for young people. Dad and I have everything we want."

The servants had found their gifts and disappeared, expressing effusive Scandinavian thanks.

Caroline and her mother were left alone.

"Mother, where did the coat come from?"

"Lloyd and Henry's."

"They keep all kinds of furs, don't they?"

"Yes."

"Would you mind horribly if I exchanged this?"

"Certainly not, dear. You pick out anything you like, and if it's a little more expensive, it won't make any difference.

We can go in town tomorrow or next day. But don't you want to wear your opals to the Murdocks'?"

"I don't believe so. They might get lost or something. And I'm not—well, I'm not so crazy about—"

"I think they can be exchanged, too," said Grace. "You run along now and get ready to start."

Caroline obeyed with alacrity, and Grace spent a welcome moment by herself.

Tom opened the garage door.

"Why, you've got two cars!" said Ted.

"The new one isn't mine," said Tom.

"Whose is it?"

"Yours. It's the new model."

"Dad, that's wonderful! But it looks just like the old one."

"Well, the old one's pretty good. Just the same, yours is better. You'll find that out when you drive it. Hop in and get started. I had her filled with gas."

"I think I'd rather drive the old one."

"Why?"

"Well, what I really wanted, Dad, was a Barnes sport roadster, something like Paul Murdock's, only a different color scheme. And if I don't drive this Gorham at all, maybe you could get them to take it back or make some kind of deal with the Barnes people."

Tom didn't speak till he was sure of his voice. Then: "All right, son. Take my car and I'll see what can be done about yours."

Caroline, waiting for Ted, remembered something and

called to her mother. "Here's what I got for you and Dad," she said. "It's two tickets to 'Jolly Jane,' the play I saw last night. You'll love it!"

"When are they for?" asked Grace.

"Tonight," said Caroline.

"But dearie," said her mother, "we don't want to go out tonight, when you promised to stay home."

"We'll keep our promise," said Caroline, "but the Murdocks may drop in and bring some friends and we'll dance and there'll be music. And Ted and I both thought you'd rather be away somewhere so our noise wouldn't disturb you."

"It was sweet of you to do this," said her mother, "but your father and I don't mind noise as long as you're enjoying yourselves."

"It's time anyway that you and Dad had a treat."

"The real treat," said Grace, "would be to spend a quiet evening here with just you two."

"The Murdocks practically invited themselves and I couldn't say no after they'd been so nice to me. And honestly, Mother, you'll love this play!"

"Will you be home for supper?"

"I'm pretty sure we will, but if we're a little late, don't you and Dad wait for us. Take the seven-twenty so you won't miss anything. The first act is really the best. We probably won't be hungry, but have Signe leave something out for us in case we are."

Tom and Grace sat down to the elaborate Christmas dinner and didn't make much impression on it. Even if they had had any appetite, the sixteen-pound turkey would have looked almost like new when they had eaten their fill. Conversation was intermittent and related chiefly to Signe's excellence as a cook and the mildness of the weather. Children and Christmas were barely touched on.

Tom merely suggested that on account of its being a holiday and their having theatre tickets, they ought to take the six-ten and eat supper at the Metropole. His wife said no; Ted and Caroline might come home and be disappointed at not finding them. Tom seemed about to make some remark, but changed his mind.

The afternoon was the longest Grace had ever known. The children were still absent at seven and she and Tom taxied to the train. Neither talked much on the way to town. As for the play, which Grace was sure to love, it turned out to be a rehash of "Cradle Snatchers" and "Sex," retaining the worst features of each.

When it was over, Tom said: "Now I'm inviting you to the Cove Club. You didn't eat any breakfast or dinner or supper and I can't have you starving to death on a feast-day. Besides, I'm thirsty as well as hungry."

They ordered the special *table d'hôte* and struggled hard to get away with it. Tom drank six high-balls, but they failed to produce the usual effect of making him jovial. Grace had one high-ball and some kind of cordial that gave her a warm, contented feeling for a moment. But the warmth and contentment left her before the train was halfway home.

The living-room looked as if Von Kluck's army had just passed through. Ted and Caroline had kept their promise up to a certain point. They had spent part of the evening at home, and the Murdocks must have brought all their own friends and everybody else's, judging from the results. The tables and floors were strewn with empty glasses, ashes and cigaret stubs. The stockings had been torn off their nails and the wrecked contents were all over the place. Two sizable holes had been burnt in Grace's favorite rug.

Tom took his wife by the arm and led her into the music-room.

"You never took the trouble to open your own present," he said.

"And I think there's one for you, too," said Grace. "They didn't come in here," she added, "so I guess there wasn't much dancing or music."

Tom found his gift from Grace, a set of diamond studs and cuff buttons for festive wear. Grace's present from him was an opal ring.

"Oh, Tom!" she said.

"We'll have to go out somewhere tomorrow night, so I can break these in," said Tom.

"Well, if we do that, we'd better get a good night's rest."

"I'll beat you upstairs," said Tom.

One Christmas Eve

LANGSTON HUGHES

Standing over the hot stove cooking supper, the colored maid, Arcie, was very tired. Between meals today, she had cleaned the whole house for the white family she worked for, getting ready for Christmas tomorrow. Now her back ached and her head felt faint from sheer fatigue. Well, she would be off in a little while, if only the Missus and her children would come on home to dinner. They were out shopping for more things for the tree which stood all ready tinsel-hung and lovely in the living-room, waiting for its candles to be lighted.

Arcie wished she could afford a tree for Joe. He'd never had one yet, and it's nice to have such things when you're little. Joe was five, going on six. Arcie, looking at the roast in the white folks' oven, wondered how much she could afford to spend tonight on toys. She only got seven dollars a week, and four of that went for her room and the landlady's daily looking after Joe while Arcie was at work.

"Lord, it's more'n a notion raisin' a child," she thought.

She looked at the clock on the kitchen table. After seven. What made white folks so darned inconsiderate? Why didn't they come on home here to supper? They knew she wanted to get off before all the stores closed. She wouldn't have time to buy Joe nothin' if they didn't hurry. And her landlady probably wanting to go out and shop, too, and not be bothered with little Joe.

"Dog gone it!" Arcie said to herself. "If I just had my money, I might leave the supper on the stove for 'em. I just got to get to the stores fo' they close." But she hadn't been paid for the week yet. The Missus had promised to pay her Christmas Eve, a day or so ahead of time.

Arcie heard a door slam and talking and laughter in the front of the house. She went in and saw the Missus and her kids shaking snow off their coats.

"Ummm-mm! It's swell for Christmas Eve," one of the kids said to Arcie. "It's snowin' like the deuce, and mother came near driving through a stop light. Can't hardly see for the snow. It's swell!"

"Supper's ready," Arcie said. She was thinking how her shoes weren't very good for walking in snow.

It seemed like the white folks took as long as they could to eat that evening. While Arcie was washing dishes, the Missus came out with her money.

"Arcie," the Missus said, "I'm so sorry, but would you mind if I just gave you five dollars tonight? The children have made me run short of change, buying presents and all."

"I'd like to have seven," Arcie said. "I needs it."

"Well, I just haven't got seven," the Missus said. "I didn't know you'd want all your money before the end of the week, anyhow. I just haven't got it to spare."

Arcie took five. Coming out of the hot kitchen, she wrapped up as well as she could and hurried by the house where she roomed to get little Joe. At least he could look at the Christmas trees in the windows downtown.

The landlady, a big light yellow woman, was in a bad humor. She said to Arcie, "I thought you was comin' home early and get this child. I guess you know I want to go out, too, once in a while."

Arcie didn't say anything for, if she had, she knew the landlady would probably throw it up to her that she wasn't getting paid to look after a child both night and day.

"Come on, Joe," Arcie said to her son, "let's us go in the street."

"I hears they got a Santa Claus downtown," Joe said, wriggling into his worn little coat. "I wants to see him."

"Don't know 'bout that," his mother said, "but hurry up and get your rubbers on. Stores'll all be closed directly."

It was six or eight blocks downtown. They trudged along through the falling snow, both of them a little cold. But the snow was pretty!

The main street was hung with bright red and blue lights.

In front of the City Hall there was a Christmas tree—but it didn't have no presents on it, only lights. In the store windows there were lots of toys—for sale.

Joe kept on saying, "Mama, I want . . ."

But mama kept walking ahead. It was nearly ten, when the stores were due to close, and Arcie wanted to get Joe some cheap gloves and something to keep him warm, as well as a toy or two. She thought she might come across a rummage sale where they had children's clothes. And in the ten-cent store, she could get some toys.

"O-oo! Lookee . . . ," little Joe kept saying, and pointing at things in the windows. How warm and pretty the lights were, and the shops, and the electric signs through the snow.

It took Arcie more than a dollar to get Joe's mittens and things he needed. In the A & P Arcie bought a big box of hard candies for 49¢. And then she guided Joe through the crowd on the street until they came to the dime store. Near the ten-cent store they passed a moving picture theatre. Joe said he wanted to go in and see the movies.

Arcie said, "Ump-un! No, child! This ain't Baltimore where they have shows for colored, too. In these here small towns, they don't let colored folks in. We can't go in there."

"Oh," said little Joe.

In the ten-cent store, there was an awful crowd. Arcie told Joe to stand outside and wait for her. Keeping hold of him in the crowded store would be a job. Besides she didn't want him to see what toys she was buying. They were to be a surprise from Santa Claus tomorrow.

Little Joe stood outside the ten-cent store in the light,

and the snow, and people passing. Gee, Christmas was pretty. All tinsel and stars and cotton. And Santa Claus a-coming from somewhere, dropping things in stockings. And all the people in the streets were carrying things, and the kids looked happy.

But Joe soon got tired of just standing and thinking and waiting in front of the ten-cent store. There were so many things to look at in the other windows. He moved along up the block a little, and then a little more, walking and looking. In fact, he moved until he came to the white folks' picture show.

In the lobby of the moving picture show, behind the plate-glass doors, it was all warm and glowing and awful pretty. Joe stood looking in, and as he looked his eyes began to make out, in there blazing beneath holly and colored streamers and the electric stars of the lobby, a marvellous Christmas tree. A group of children and grown-ups, white, of course, were standing around a big jovial man in red beside the tree. Or was it a man? Little Joe's eyes opened wide. No, it was not a man at all. It was Santa Claus!

Little Joe pushed open one of the glass doors and ran into the lobby of the white moving picture show. Little Joe went right through the crowd and up to where he could get a good look at Santa Claus. And Santa Claus was giving away gifts, little presents for children, little boxes of animal crackers and stick-candy canes. And behind him on the tree was a big sign (which little Joe didn't know how to read). It said, to those who understood, MERRY XMAS FROM SANTA CLAUS TO OUR YOUNG PATRONS.

Around the lobby, other signs said, WHEN YOU COME OUT OF THE SHOW STOP WITH YOUR CHILDREN AND SEE OUR SANTA CLAUS. And another announced, GEM THEATRE MAKES ITS CUSTOMERS HAPPY—SEE OUR SANTA.

And there was Santa Claus in a red suit and a white beard all sprinkled with tinsel snow. Around him were rattles and drums and rocking horses which he was not giving away. But the signs on them said (could little Joe have read) that they would be presented from the stage on Christmas Day to the holders of the lucky numbers. Tonight, Santa Claus was only giving away candy, and stick-candy canes, and animal crackers to the kids.

Joe would have liked terribly to have a stick-candy cane. He came a little closer to Santa Claus, until he was right in the front of the crowd. And then Santa Claus saw Joe.

Why is it that lots of white people always grin when they see a Negro child? Santa Claus grinned. Everybody else grinned, too, looking at little black Joe—who had no business in the lobby of a white theatre. Then Santa Claus stooped down and slyly picked up one of his lucky number rattles, a great big loud tin-pan rattle such as they use in cabarets. And he shook it fiercely right at Joe. That was funny. The white people laughed, kids and all. But little Joe didn't laugh. He was scared. To the shaking of the big rattle, he turned and fled out of the warm lobby of the threatre, out into the street where the snow was and the people. Frightened by laughter, he had begun to cry. He went looking for his mama. In his heart he never thought Santa Claus shook great rattles at children like that—and then laughed.

In the crowd on the street he went the wrong way. He couldn't find the ten-cent store or his mother. There were too many people, all white people, moving like white shadows in the snow, a world of white people.

It seemed to Joe an awfully long time till he suddenly saw Arcie, dark and worried-looking, cut across the sidewalk through the passing crowd and grab him. Although her arms were full of packages, she still managed with one free hand to shake him until his teeth rattled.

"Why didn't you stand where I left you?" Arcie demanded loudly. "Tired as I am, I got to run all over the streets in the night lookin' for you. I'm a great mind to wear you out."

When little Joe got his breath back, on the way home, he told his mama he had been in the moving picture show.

"But Santa Claus didn't give me nothin'," Joe said tearfully. "He made a big noise at me and I runned out."

"Serves you right," said Arcie, trudging through the snow. "You had no business in there. I told you to stay where I left you."

"But I seed Santa Claus in there," little Joe said, "so I went in."

"Huh! That wasn't no Santa Claus," Arcie explained. "If it was, he wouldn't a-treated you like that. That's a threatre for white folks—I told you once—and he's just a old white man."

"Oh . . . ," said little Joe.

The Burglar's Christmas

WILLA CATHER

Two very shabby-looking young men stood at the corner of Prairie Avenue and Eightieth Street, looking despondently at the carriages that whirled by. It was Christmas Eve, and the streets were full of vehicles; florists' wagons, grocers' carts, and carriages. The streets were in that half-liquid, half-congealed condition peculiar to the streets of Chicago at that season of the year. The swift wheels that spun by sometimes threw the slush of mud and snow over the two young men who were talking on the corner.

"Well," remarked the elder of the two, "I guess we are at our rope's end, sure enough. How do you feel?"

"Pretty shaky. The wind's sharp tonight. If I had had anything to eat I mightn't mind it so much. There is simply no show. I'm sick of the whole business. Looks like there's nothing for it but the lake."

"Oh, nonsense, I thought you had more grit. Got anything left you can hock?"

"Nothing but my beard, and I am afraid they wouldn't find it worth a pawn ticket," said the younger man ruefully, rubbing the week's growth of stubble on his face.

"Got any folks anywhere? Now's your time to strike 'em if you have."

"Never mind if I have, they're out of the question."

"Well, you'll be out of it before many hours if you don't make a move of some sort. A man's got to eat. See here, I am going down to Longtin's saloon. I used to play the banjo in there, and I'll bone him for some of his free-lunch stuff. You'd better come along; perhaps they'll fill an order for two."

"How far down is it?"

"Well, it's clear downtown, of course, way down on Michigan Avenue."

"Thanks, I guess I'll loaf around here. I don't feel equal to the walk, and the cars—well, the cars are crowded." His features drew themselves into what might have been a smile under happier circumstances.

"No, you never did like streetcars, you're too aristocratic. See here, Crawford, I don't like leaving you here. You ain't good company for yourself tonight."

"Crawford? Oh yes, that's the last one. There have been so many I forget them."

"Have you got a real name, anyway?"

"Oh yes, but it's one of the ones I've forgotten. Don't you worry about me. You go along and get your free lunch. I think I had a row in Longtin's place once. I'd better not show myself there again." As he spoke the young man nodded and turned slowly up the avenue.

He was miserable enough to want to be quite alone. Even the crowd that jostled by him annoyed him. He wanted to think about himself. He had avoided this final reckoning with himself for a year now. He had laughed it off and drunk it off. But now, when all those artificial devices which are employed to turn our thoughts into other channels and shield us from ourselves had failed him, it must come. Hunger is a powerful incentive to introspection.

It is a tragic hour, that hour when we are finally driven to reckon with ourselves, when every avenue of mental distraction has been cut off and our own life and all its ineffaceable failures closes about us like the walls of that old torture chamber of the Inquisition. Tonight, as this man stood stranded in the streets of the city, his hour came. It was not the first time he had been hungry and desperate and alone. But always before there had been some outlook, some chance ahead, some pleasure yet untasted that seemed worth the effort, some face that he fancied was, or would be, dear. But it was not so tonight. The unyielding conviction was upon him that he had failed in everything, had outlived everything. It had been near him for a long time, that Pale Specter. He had caught its shadow at the bottom of his glass many a time, at the head of his bed when he was sleepless at night, in the twilight shadows when some great sunset broke upon him. It had made life hateful to him when he awoke in the morning before now. But now it settled slowly over him, like night, the endless Northern nights that bid the sun a long farewell. It rose up before him like granite. From this brilliant city with its glad bustle of Yuletide he was shut off as completely as though he were a creature of another species. His days seemed numbered and done, sealed over like the little coral cells at the bottom of the sea. Involuntarily he drew that cold air through his lungs slowly, as though he was tasting it for the last time.

Yet he was but four and twenty, this man—he looked even younger—and he had a father someplace down East who had been very proud of him once. Well, he had taken his life into his own hands, and this was what he had made of it. That was all there to be said. He could remember the hopeful things they used to say about him at college in the old days, before he had cut away and begun to live by his wits, and he found courage to smile at them now. They had read him wrongly. He knew now that he never had the essentials of success, only the superficial agility that is often mistaken for it. He was tow without the tinder, and he had burnt himself out at other people's fires. He had helped other people to make it win, but he himself—he had never touched an enterprise that had not failed eventually. Or, if it survived his connection with it, it left him behind.

His last venture had been with some ten-cent specialty company, a little lower than all the others, that had gone to pieces in Buffalo, and he had worked his way to Chicago by boat. When the boat made up its crew for the outward voyage, he was dispensed with as usual. He was used to that. The reason for it? Oh, there are so many reasons for failure! His was a very common one.

As he stood there in the wet under the street light he drew up his reckoning with the world and decided that it had treated him as well as he deserved. He had overdrawn his account once too often. There had been a day when he thought otherwise—when he had said he was unjustly handled, that his failure was merely the lack of proper adjustment between himself and other men, that someday he would be recognized and it would all come right. But he knew better than that now, and he was still man enough to bear no grudge against anyone—man or woman.

Tonight was his birthday, too. There seemed something particularly amusing in that. He turned up a limp little coat collar to try to keep a little of the wet chill from his throat and instinctively began to remember all the birthday parties he used to have. He was so cold and empty that his mind seemed unable to grapple with any serious question. He kept thinking about gingerbread and frosted cakes like a child. He could remember the splendid birthday parties his mother used to give him, when all the other little boys in the block came in their Sunday clothes and creaking shoes, with their ears still red from their mother's towel, and the pink and white birthday cake, and the stuffed olives and all the dishes of which he had been particularly fond, and how he would eat and eat and then go to bed and dream of Santa Claus. And in the morning he would awaken and eat again, until by night the family doctor arrived with his castor oil, and poor William used to dolefully say that it was altogether too much to have your birthday and Christmas all at once. He could remember, too, the royal birthday suppers he had given at college, and the stag dinners, and the toasts, and the music, and the good fellows who had wished him happiness and really meant what they said.

And since then there were other birthday suppers that he could not remember so clearly; the memory of them was heavy and flat, like cigarette smoke that has been shut in a room all night, like champagne that has been a day opened, a song that has been too often sung, an acute sensation that has been overstrained. They seemed tawdry and garish, discordant to him now. He rather wished he could forget them altogether.

Whichever way his mind now turned there was one thought that it could not escape, and that was the idea of food. He caught the scent of a cigar suddenly, and felt a sharp pain in the pit of his abdomen and a sudden moisture in his mouth. His cold hands clenched angrily, and for a moment he felt that bitter hatred of wealth, of ease, of everything that is well fed and well housed that is common to starving men. At any rate he had a right to eat! He had demanded great things from the world once: fame and wealth and admiration. Now it was simply bread—and he would have it! He looked about him quickly and felt the blood begin to stir in his veins. In all his straits he had never stolen anything, his tastes were above it. But tonight there would be no tomorrow. He was amused at the way in which the idea excited him. Was it possible there was yet one more experience that would distract him, one thing that had power to excite his jaded interest? Good! He had failed at everything else, now he would see what his chances would be as a common thief. It would be amusing to watch the beautiful consistency of his destiny work itself out even in that role. It would be interesting to add another study to his gallery of futile attempts, and then label them all: "The failure as a journalist," "The failure as a lecturer," "The failure as a businessman," "The failure as a thief," and so on, like the titles under the pictures of the Dance of Death. It was time that Childe Roland came to the dark tower.

A girl hastened by him with her arms full of packages. She walked quickly and nervously, keeping well within the shadow, as if she were not accustomed to carrying bundles and did not care to meet any of her friends. As she crossed the muddy street, she made an effort to lift her skirt a little, and as she did so one of the packages slipped unnoticed from beneath her arm. He caught it up and overtook her. "Excuse me, but I think you dropped something."

She started, "Oh yes, thank you, I would rather have lost anything than that."

The young man turned angrily upon himself. The package must have contained something of value. Why had he not kept it? Was this the sort of thief he would make? He ground his teeth together. There is nothing more maddening than to have morally consented to crime and then lack the nerve force to carry it out.

A carriage drove up to the house before which he stood.

Several richly dressed women alighted and went in. It was a new house, and must have been built since he was in Chicago last. The front door was open and he could see down the hallway and up the staircase. The servant had left the door and gone with the guests. The first floor was brilliantly lighted, but the windows upstairs were dark. It looked very easy, just to slip upstairs to the darkened chambers where the jewels and trinkets of the fashionable occupants were kept.

Still burning with impatience against himself he entered quickly. Instinctively he removed his mud-stained hat as he passed quickly and quietly up the staircase. It struck him as being a rather superfluous courtesy in a burglar, but he had done it before he had thought. His way was clear enough, he met no one on the stairway or in the upper hall. The gas was lit in the upper hall. He passed the first chamber door through sheer cowardice. The second he entered quickly, thinking of something else lest his courage should fail him, and closed the door behind him. The light from the hall shone into the room through the transom. The apartment was finished richly enough to justify his expectations. He went at once to the dressing case. A number of rings and small trinkets lay in a silver tray. These he put hastily in his pocket. He opened the upper drawer and found, as he expected, several leather cases. In the first he opened was a lady's watch, in the second a pair of old-fashioned bracelets; he seemed to dimly remember having seen bracelets like them before, somewhere. The third case was heavier, the spring was much worn, and it opened easily. It held a cup of some kind. He held it up to the light and then his strained nerves gave way and he uttered a sharp exclamation. It was the silver mug he used to drink from when he was a little boy.

The door opened, and a woman stood in the doorway facing him. She was a tall woman, with white hair, in evening dress. The light from the hall streamed in upon him, but she was not afraid. She stood looking at him a moment, then she threw out her hand and went quickly toward him.

"Willie, Willie! Is it you?"

He struggled to loose her arms from him, to keep her lips from his cheek. "Mother—you must not! You do not understand! Oh, my God, this is worst of all!" Hunger, weakness, cold, shame, all came back to him, and shook his self-control completely. Physically he was too weak to stand a shock like this. Why could it not have been an ordinary discovery, arrest, the station house and all the rest of it. Anything but this! A hard dry sob broke from him. Again he strove to disengage himself.

"Who is it says I shall not kiss my son? Oh, my boy, we have waited so long for this! You have been so long in coming, even I almost gave you up."

Her lips upon his cheek burnt him like fire. He put his hand to his throat, and spoke thickly and incoherently: "You do not understand. I did not know you were here. I came here to rob—it is the first time—I swear it—but I am a common thief. My pockets are full of your jewels now. Can't you hear me? I am a common thief!"

"Hush, my boy, those are ugly words. How could you rob your own house? How could you take what is your own? They are all yours, my son, as wholly yours as my great love—and you can't doubt that, Will, do you?"

That soft voice, the warmth and fragrance of her person stole through his chill, empty veins like a gentle stimulant. He felt as though all his strength were leaving him and even consciousness. He held fast to her and bowed his head on her strong shoulder, and groaned aloud.

"O, Mother, life is hard, hard!"

She said nothing, but held him closer. And oh, the strength of those white arms that held him! Oh, the assurance of safety in that warm bosom that rose and fell under his cheek! For a moment they stood so, silently. Then they heard a heavy step upon the stair. She led him to a chair and went out and closed the door. At the top of the staircase she met a tall, broad-shouldered man, with iron-gray hair, and a face alert and stern. Her eyes were shining and her cheeks on fire, her whole face was one expression of intense determination.

"James, it is William in there, come home. You must keep him at any cost. If he goes this time, I go with him. Oh, James, be easy with him, he has suffered so." She broke from a command to an entreaty, and laid her hand on his shoulder. He looked questioningly at her a moment, then went in the room and quietly shut the door.

She stood leaning against the wall, clasping her temples with her hands and listening to the low indistinct sound of the voices within. Her own lips moved silently. She waited a long time, scarcely breathing. At last the door opened, and her husband came out. He stopped to say in a shaken voice,

"You go to him now, he will stay. I will go to my room. I will see him again in the morning."

She put her arm about his neck, "Oh, James, I thank you, I thank you! This is the night he came so long ago, you remember? I gave him to you then, and now you give him back to me!"

"Don't, Helen," he muttered. "He is my son, I have never forgotten that. I failed with him. I don't like to fail, it cuts my pride. Take him and make a man of him." He passed on down the hall.

She flew into the room where the young man sat with his head bowed upon his knee. She dropped to her knees beside him. Ah, it was so good to him to feel those arms again!

"He is so glad, Willie, so glad! He may not show it, but he is as happy as I. He never was demonstrative with either of us, you know."

"Oh my God, he was good enough," groaned the man. "I told him everything, and he was good enough. I don't see how either of you can look at me, speak to me, touch me." He shivered under her clasp again as when she had first touched him, and tried weakly to throw her off.

But she whispered softly, "This is my right, my son."

Presently, when he was calmer, she rose. "Now, come with me into the library, and I will have your dinner brought there."

As they went downstairs she remarked apologetically, "I will not call Ellen tonight; she has a number of guests to attend to. She is a big girl now, you know, and came out last winter. Besides, I want you all to myself tonight."

When the dinner came, and it came very soon, he fell upon it savagely. As he ate she told him all that had transpired during the years of his absence, and how his father's business had brought them there. "I was glad when we came. I thought you would drift West. I seemed a good deal nearer to you here."

There was a gentle unobtrusive sadness in her tone that was too soft for a reproach.

"Have you everything you want? It is a comfort to see you eat."

He smiled grimly. "It is certainly a comfort to me. I have not indulged in this frivolous habit for some thirty-five hours."

She caught his hand and pressed it sharply, uttering a quick remonstrance.

"Don't say that! I know, but I can't hear you say it—it's too terrible! My boy, food has choked me many a time when I have thought of the possibility of that. Now take the old lounging chair by the fire, and if you are too tired to talk, we will just sit and rest together."

He sank into the depths of the big leather chair with the lions' heads on the arms, where he had sat so often in the days when his feet did not touch the floor and he was half afraid of the grim monsters cut in the polished wood. That chair seemed to speak to him of things long forgotten. It was like the touch of an old familiar friend. He felt a sudden yearning tenderness for the happy little boy who had sat there and dreamed of the big world so long ago. Alas, he had been dead many a summer, that little boy!

He sat looking up at the magnificent woman beside him. He had almost forgotten how handsome she was; how lustrous and sad were the eyes that set under that serene brow, how impetuous and wayward the mouth even now, how superb the white throat and shoulders! Ah, the wit and grace and fineness of this woman! He remembered how proud he had been of her as a boy when she came to see him at school. Then in the deep red coals of the grate he saw the faces of other women who had come since then into his vexed, disordered life. Laughing faces, with eyes artificially bright, eyes without depth or meaning, features without the stamp of high sensibilities. And he had left this face for such as those!

He sighed restlessly and laid his hand on hers. There seemed refuge and protection in the touch of her, as in the old days when he was afraid of the dark. He had been in the dark so long now, his confidence was so thoroughly shaken, and he was bitterly afraid of the night and of himself.

"Ah, Mother, you make other things seem so false. You must feel that I owe you an explanation, but I can't make any, even to myself. Ah, but we make poor exchanges in life. I can't make out the riddle of it all. Yet there are things I ought to tell you before I accept your confidence like this."

"I'd rather you wouldn't, Will. Listen: Between you and me there can be no secrets. We are more alike than other people. Dear boy, I know all about it. I am a woman, and circumstances were different with me, but we are of one blood. I have lived all your life before you. You have never had an impulse that I have not known, you have never touched a brink that my feet have not trod. This is your birthday night. Twenty-four years ago I foresaw all this. I was a young woman then and I had hot battles of my own, and I felt your likeness to me. You were not like other babies. From the hour you were born you were restless and discontented, as I had been before you. You used to brace your strong little limbs against mine and try to throw me off as you did tonight. Tonight you have come back to me, just as you always did after you ran away to swim in the river that was forbidden you, the river you loved because it was forbidden. You are tired and sleepy, just as you used to be then, only a little older and a little paler and a little more foolish. I never asked you where you had been then, nor will I now. You have come back to me, that's all in all to me. I know your every possibility and limitation, as a composer knows his instrument."

He found no answer that was worthy to give to talk like this. He had not found life easy since he had lived by his wits. He had come to know poverty at close quarters. He had known what it was to be gay with an empty pocket, to wear violets in his buttonhole when he had not breakfasted, and all the hateful shams of the poverty of idleness. He had been a reporter on a big metropolitan daily, where men grind out their brains on paper until they have not one idea left—and still grind on. He had worked in a real estate office, where ignorant men were swindled. He had sung in a comic opera chorus, and played Harris in an *Uncle Tom's Cabin* company, and edited a socialist weekly. He had been dogged by debt and hunger and grinding poverty, until to sit here by a warm fire without concern as to how it would be paid for seemed unnatural.

He looked up at her questioningly. "I wonder if you know how much you pardon?"

"Oh, my poor boy, much or little, what does it matter? Have you wandered so far and paid such a bitter price for knowledge and not yet learned that love has nothing to do with pardon or forgiveness, that it only loves, and loves—and loves? They have not taught you well, the women of your world." She leaned over and kissed him, as no woman had kissed him since he left her.

He drew a long sigh of rich content. The old life, with all its bitterness and useless antagonism and flimsy sophistries, its brief delights that were always tinged with fear and distrust and unfaith, that whole miserable, futile, swindled world of Bohemia seemed immeasurably distant and far away, like a dream that is over and done. And as the chimes rang joyfully outside and sleep pressed heavily upon his eyelids, he wondered dimly if the Author of this sad little riddle of ours were not able to solve it after all, and if the Potter would not finally mete out his all comprehensive justice, such as none but he could have, to his Things of Clay, which are made in his own patterns, weak or strong, for his own ends; and if some day we will not awaken and find that all evil is a dream, a mental distortion that will pass when the dawn shall break.

from WASHINGTON IRVING'S

The Sketch Book

It is a beautiful arrangement, that this festival, which commemorates the announcement of the religion of peace and love, has been made the season for gathering together of family connections, and drawing closer again those bands of kindred hearts which the cares and pleasures and sorrows of the world are continually operating to cast loose; of calling back the children of a family who have launched forth in life, once more to assemble about the paternal hearth, that rallying-place of the affections, there to grow young and loving again among the endearing mementos of childhood.

It is, indeed, the season of regenerated feeling—the season for kindling, not merely the fire of hospitality in the hall, but the genial flame of charity in the heart.

O Little Town of Bethlehem

O little town of Bethlehem,
How still we see thee lie!
Above thy deep and dreamless sleep
The silent stars go by:
Yet in thy dark streets shineth
The everlasting Light;
The hopes and fears of all the years
Are met in thee tonight.

For Christ is born of Mary;
And gathered all above,
While mortals sleep, the angels keep
Their watch of wondering love.
O morning stars together
Proclaim thy holy birth;
And praises sing to God the King,
And peace to men on earth.

How silently, how silently,
The wondrous Gift is given!
So God imparts to human hearts
The blessing of His heaven.
No ear may hear His coming,
But in this world of sin,
Where meek souls will receive Him still,
The dear Christ enters in.

O holy Child of Bethlehem,
Descend to us, we pray;
Cast out our sins, and enter in,
Be born in us today.
We hear the Christmas angels
The great glad tidings tell;
O come to us, abide with us,
Our Lord Emmanuel.

PHILLIPS BROOKS

Silent Night

Silent night, holy night!
  All is calm, all is bright
'Round yon Virgin Mother and Child—
  Holy infant, so tender and mild.
Sleep in heavenly peace,
Sleep in heavenly peace.

Silent night, holy night!
  Shepherds quake at the sight.
Glories stream from Heaven afar,
  Heav'nly hosts sing "Alleluia,
Christ the Savior is born,
Christ the Savior is born!"

Silent night, holy night!
  Son of God, love's pure light,
Radiance beams from Thy holy face,
  With the dawn of redeeming grace.
Jesus, Lord at Thy birth,
Jesus, Lord at Thy birth!

JOSEPH MOHR

from

ALFRED, LORD TENNYSON'S

In Memoriam

The time draws near the birth of Christ:
  The moon is hid; the night is still;
  The Christmas bells from hill to hill
Answer each other in the mist.

Four voices of four hamlets round,
  From far and near, on mead and moor,
  Swell out and fail, as if a door
Were shut between me and the sound:

Each voice four changes on the wind,
  That now dilate, and now decrease,
  Peace and good will, good will and peace,
Peace and good will, to all mankind.

O Come, All Ye Faithful

O come, all ye faithful,
Joyful and triumphant;
O come ye, O come ye to Bethlehem;
Come and behold Him
Born the King of angels;

O come, let us adore Him,
O come, let us adore Him,
O come, let us adore Him,
Christ the Lord.

Sing, choirs of angels,
Sing in exultation,
Sing all ye citizens of heav'n above:
Glory to God
In the highest.

O come, let us adore Him,
O come, let us adore Him,
O come, let us adore Him,
Christ the Lord.

Yea Lord, we greet Thee,
Born this happy morning;
Jesus to Thee be glory giv'n;

Word of the Father,
Now in flesh appearing.

O come, let us adore Him,
O come, let us adore Him,
O come, let us adore Him,
Christ the Lord.

TRADITIONAL CAROL

A Christmas Carmen

Sound over all waters, reach out from all lands,
The chorus of voices, the clasping of hands;
Sing hymns that were sung by the stars of the morn,
Sing songs of the angels when Jesus was born!
With glad jubilations
Bring hope to the nations!
The dark night is ending and dawn has begun:
Rise, hope of the ages, arise like the sun,
All speech flow to music, all hearts beat as one!

Sing the bridal of nations! with chorals of love
Sing out the war-vulture and sing in the dove,
Till the hearts of the peoples keep time in accord,
And the voice of the world is the voice of the Lord!
Clasp hands of the nations
In strong gratulations:
The dark night is ending and dawn has begun;
Rise, hope of the ages, arise like the sun,
All speech flow to music, all hearts beat as one.

Blow, bugles of battle, the marches of peace;
East, west, north, and south let the long quarrel cease:
Sing the song of great joy that the angels began,
Sing of glory to God and of good-will to man!

Hark! joining in chorus
The heavens bend o'er us!
The dark night is ending and dawn has begun;
Rise, hope of the ages, arise like the sun,
All speech flow to music, all hearts beat as one!

JOHN GREENLEAF WHITTIER

Christmas Everywhere

Everywhere, everywhere, Christmas tonight!
Christmas in lands of the fir-tree and pine,
Christmas in lands of the palm-tree and vine,
Christmas where snow peaks stand solemn and white,
Christmas where cornfields stand sunny and bright.
Christmas where children are hopeful and gay,
Christmas where old men are patient and gray,
Christmas where peace, like a dove in his flight,
Broods o'er brave men in the thick of the fight;
Everywhere, everywhere, Christmas tonight!
For the Christ-child who comes is the Master of all;
No palace too great, no cottage too small.

PHILLIPS BROOKS

This Is Christmas

The evergreen singing aloud its poem of constant renewal,
The festive mood spreading lilting magic everywhere,
The gifts of recollection calling to heart the graces of life,
The star in the sky calling to mind the wisdom of hope,
The warmth of candlelight glowing against the darkness,
The birth of a child linking past to future,
The symbol of love absorbing all violence.

THIS IS CHRISTMAS

HOWARD THURMAN

Joy to the World

Joy to the world! The Lord is come.
Let Earth receive her King.
Let ev'ry heart prepare Him room,
And Heav'n and Nature sing,
And Heav'n and Nature sing,
And Heav'n, and Heav'n and Nature sing.

Joy to the world! The Savior reigns.
Let men their songs employ,
While fields and floods, rocks, hills, and plains
Repeat the sounding joy,
Repeat the sounding joy,
Repeat, repeat the sounding joy.

He rules the world with truth and grace
And makes the nations prove
The glories of His righteousness
And wonders of His love,
And wonders of His love,
And wonders, wonders of His love.

ISAAC WATTS

Recipes

from Fannie Merritt Farmer's

THE BOSTON
COOKING-SCHOOL
COOK BOOK

(Originally published in 1896)

Roast Beef

Wipe, put on a rack in dripping-pan, skin side down, rub over with salt, and dredge meat and pan with flour. Place in a hot oven (400°F), that the surface may be quickly seared, thus preventing escape of inner juices. After flour in pan is browned, reduce heat to 350°F, and baste occasionally with drippings. When meat is about half done, turn it over and dredge with flour, that skin side may be uppermost for final browning. Roasting time should be at least one and one half hours for every ten pounds of beef. Beef to be well roasted should be started in hot oven and heat decreased, so that when carved the slices will be red throughout, with a crisp layer of golden brown fat on the top.

Roast Beef Gravy

Remove some of the fat from pan, leaving four tablespoons. Place on front of range, add four tablespoons flour, and stir until well browned. The flour, dredged and browned in pan, should give additional color to gravy. Add gradually one and one-half cups boiling water, cook five minutes, season with salt and pepper, and strain.

Yorkshire Pudding

1 cup milk
1 cup flour
2 eggs
¼ teaspoon salt

Mix salt and flour, and add milk gradually to form a smooth paste; then add eggs beaten until very light. Cover bottom of hot pan with some beef drippings from the roast, and pour mixture in pan one-half inch deep. Bake twenty minutes in hot oven (400°F), basting after well-risen, with some of the fat from pan in which meat is roasting. Cut in squares for serving.

Potatoes Baked in Half-Shell

Select smooth, medium-sized potatoes. Wash, using a vegetable brush, and place in dripping-pan. Bake in hot oven (400°F) forty minutes or until soft. Remove from oven, cut slice from side of each, and scoop out inside. Mash, add two tablespoons butter, salt, pepper, and three tablespoons hot milk; then add whites of two eggs well-beaten. Refill skins, and bake five to eight minutes in very hot oven (425°F). Potatoes may be sprinkled with grated cheese before putting in oven.

Waldorf Salad

Mix equal quantities of finely cut apple and celery, and moisten with mayonnaise dressing. Garnish with curled celery and canned pimentoes cut in strips or fancy shapes. An attractive way of serving this salad is to remove the tops from red or green apples and scoop out inside pulp, leaving just enough adhering to skin to keep apples in shape. Refill shells thus made with the salad, replace tops, and serve on lettuce leaves.

Mashed Turnips

Wash and pare turnips, cut in slices or quarters, and cook in boiling salted water until soft. Drain, mash, and season with butter, salt, and pepper.

Harvard Beets

Wash twelve small beets, cook in boiling water until soft. Remove skins, and cut beets in thin slices, small cubes, or fancy shapes, using French vegetable cutter. Mix one-half cup sugar and one-half tablespoon cornstarch. Add one-half cup vinegar and let boil five minutes. Pour over beets, and let stand on back of range one-half hour. Just before serving add two tablespoons butter.

Apple Sauce

Wipe, quarter, core, and pare eight sour apples. Make a syrup by boiling seven minutes one cup sugar and one cup water with thin shaving from rind of a lemon. Remove lemon, add enough apples to cover bottom of saucepan, watch carefully during cooking, and remove as soon as soft. Continue until all are cooked. Strain remaining syrup over apples.

Roast Turkey

Dress, clean, stuff, and truss a ten-pound turkey. Place on its side on rack in a dripping-pan, rub entire surface with salt, and spread breast, legs, and wings with one-third cup butter, rubbed until creamy and mixed with one-fourth cup flour. Dredge bottom of pan with flour. Place in a hot oven (400°F), and when flour on turkey begins to brown, reduce heat to 350°F, and baste every fifteen minutes until turkey is cooked, which will require about three hours. For basting use one-half cup butter melted in one-half cup boiling water and after this is used baste with fat in pan. Pour water in pan during the cooking as needed to prevent flour from burning. During cooking turn turkey frequently, that it may brown evenly. If turkey is browning too fast, cover with buttered paper to prevent burning. Remove string and skewers before serving. Garnish with parsley, or celery tips, or curled celery and rings and discs of carrots strung on fine wire.

Chestnut Stuffing

3 CUPS FRENCH CHESTNUTS
½ CUP BUTTER
1 TEASPOON SALT
⅛ TEASPOON PEPPER
¼ CUP CREAM
1 CUP CRACKER CRUMBS

Shell and blanch chestnuts. Cook in boiling salted water until soft. Drain and mash, using a potato ricer. Add one-half the butter, salt, pepper, and cream. Melt remaining butter, mix with cracker crumbs, then combine mixtures.

Turkey Gravy

Pour off liquid in pan in which turkey has been roasted. From liquid skim off six tablespoons fat; return fat to pan and brown with six tablespoons flour; pour on gradually three cups stock in which giblets, neck, and tips of wings have been cooked, or use liquor left in pan. Cook five minutes, season with salt and pepper; strain. For Giblet Gravy add to the above, giblets (heart, liver, and gizzard) finely chopped.

Plum Pudding

½ LB. STALE BREAD CRUMBS
1 CUP SCALDED MILK
¼ LB. SUGAR
4 EGGS
¼ LB. RAISINS, SEEDED, CUT IN PIECES, AND FLOURED
¼ LB. CURRANTS
¼ LB. FINELY CHOPPED FIGS
2 OZ. FINELY CUT CITRON
½ LB. SUET
¼ CUP WINE AND BRANDY MIXED
½ TEASPOON GRATED NUTMEG
¾ TEASPOON CINNAMON
⅓ TEASPOON CLOVE
⅓ TEASPOON MACE
1½ TEASPOONS SALT

Soak bread crumbs in milk, let stand until cool, add sugar, beaten yolks of eggs, raisins, currants, figs, and citron; chop suet, and cream by using the hand; combine mixtures, then add wine, brandy, nutmeg, cinnamon, clove, mace, and whites of eggs beaten stiff. Turn into buttered mold, cover, and steam six hours. Serve with Hard and Liquid Sauce.

HARD SAUCE. Cream one-third cup butter; add gradually one cup brown sugar and two tablespoons brandy, drop by drop. Force through a pastry bag with rose tube, and garnish with green leaves and candied cherries.

LIQUID SAUCE. Mix one-half cup sugar, one-half tablespoon corn-starch, and a few grains salt. Add gradually, while stirring constantly, one cup boiling water, and boil five minutes. Remove from fire, add one tablespoon lemon juice and two tablespoons brandy; then color with fruit red.

Glazed Sweet Potatoes

Wash and pare six medium-sized potatoes. Cook in boiling salted water until soft. Drain, cut in halves lengthwise, and put in a buttered pan. Make a syrup by boiling three minutes one-half cup sugar and four tablespoons water; add one tablespoon butter. Brush potatoes with syrup and bake until brown, basting twice with remaining syrup.

Cranberry Sauce

Pick over and wash three cups cranberries. Put in a stewpan, add one and one-fourth cups sugar and one cup boiling water, and boil ten minutes. Care must be taken that they do not boil over. Skim and cool.

Christmas Gingerbread

- 1 LB. FLOUR
- ½ LB. BUTTER
- 1 CUP SUGAR
- 1 TABLESPOON GINGER
- 1 TEASPOON SALT
- MOLASSES

Mix flour, sugar, ginger, and salt. Work in butter, using tips of fingers, and add just enough molasses to hold ingredients together. Let stand over night to get thoroughly chilled. Roll very thin, shape, and bake in a moderate oven (350°F) for eight to ten minutes.

Coconut Cream Cookies

2 EGGS
1 CUP SUGAR
1 CUP THICK CREAM
½ CUP SHREDDED COCONUT
3 CUPS FLOUR
3 TEASPOONS BAKING POWDER
1 TEASPOON SALT

Beat eggs until light, add sugar gradually, coconut, cream, and flour mixed and sifted with baking powder and salt. Chill thoroughly, toss on a floured board, pat, and roll one-half inch thick. Sprinkle with coconut, roll one-fourth inch thick, and shape with a small round cutter, first dipped in flour. Bake on a buttered sheet in a moderate oven (350°F) for eight to ten minutes.

Chocolate Caramels

2½ TABLESPOONS BUTTER
2 CUPS MOLASSES
1 CUP BROWN SUGAR
½ CUP MILK
3 SQUARES UNSWEETENED CHOCOLATE
1 TEASPOON VANILLA

Put butter into kettle; when melted, add molasses, sugar, and milk. Stir until sugar is dissolved, and when boiling-point is reached, add chocolate, stirring constantly until chocolate is melted. Boil until, when tried in cold water, a firm ball may be formed in the fingers. Add vanilla just after taking from fire. Turn into a buttered pan, cool, and mark in small squares.

Fruit Cake

1 LB. BUTTER
1 LB. LIGHT BROWN SUGAR
9 EGGS
1 LB. FLOUR
2 TEASPOONS MACE
2 TEASPOONS CINNAMON
1 TEASPOON SODA
2 TABLESPOONS MILK
3 LBS. CURRANTS
2 LBS. RAISINS, SEEDED AND FINELY CHOPPED
½ LB. ALMONDS, BLANCHED AND SHREDDED
1 LB. CITRON, THINLY SLICED AND CUT IN STRIPS

Cream the butter, add sugar gradually, and beat thoroughly. Separate yolks from whites of eggs; beat yolks until thick and lemon-colored, whites until stiff and dry, and add to first mixture. Then add milk, fruit, nuts, and flour mixed and sifted with mace, cinnamon, and soda. Put in buttered deep pans, cover with buttered paper, steam three hours, and bake one and one half hours in a slow oven (300°F), or bake four hours in a very slow oven (275°F). Rich fruit cake is always more satisfactory when done if the cooking is accomplished by steaming.